THE HARLEQUIN

The Fae Court

Book 3

ALEXIS BROOKE

Editing - Quinn Nichols - Quill & Bone Editing

Cover Design - Krafigs Design

ISBN

Paperback - 978-1-916671-36-2

Hardback - 978-1-916671-37-9

Sometimes you don't need the villain to burn the world down for you, you just need them to pass you the matches....

ONE

Finn

FOUR MONTHS AGO

I SLIDE THE SCARLET MASK ONTO THE BRIDGE OF MY NOSE and draw back my shoulders, flexing my wings. My muscles twitch and tense with anticipation.

Because I know I am finally going to see her.

After all these years, I will be within touching distance of the woman who will change everything.

And she has no idea what's about to happen to her.

Crouching by the stream, I trail a long, lithe finger through the gently flowing water. My upper lip curls into a smile as I picture Lord Eldrion, my master, my keeper, pacing his chambers.

"Tonight is the night, Finn. Find her for me. Bring her here."

His entire body was vibrating with tension. He too craves Alana. But it would never occur to him that I am already plotting to steal her from him.

Tonight, he has given me a slice of freedom and he believes that, like a well-trained hound, I will return to him with the prey he sent me to fetch. Tail wagging. Tongue out. Desperate for his approval.

He thinks I will drop Alana at his feet and let him claim her for his own.

But he has always underestimated me.

The all-powerful Eldrion. He looks at me and sees my impotent wings, the way they almost disappear in the sunlight, their shadowy veins betraying the void inside me where magic should beat, and sing, and live.

He sees the way I bow my head, and nod, and clasp my hands behind my back as if they are physically chained there. He hears the bells that chime when I move, and thinks I will bow to him forever.

But he does not see inside my mind.

Despite all his games, and his power, he does not own that part of me.

He does not know the thoughts that have tormented me for centuries. He has no idea that I remember what he did.

I was only a child when Eldrion shattered my entire world and planted the seed of vengeance in my soul.

My parents were brave, courageous leaders amongst the Shadowkind. They dreamed of a better life for our people, free from the tyranny of the Sunborne. In secret, they gathered allies and planned a rebellion.

But they underestimated Eldrion's reach. The night before the uprising, his forces descended on our home like a plague of locusts. They dragged us from the Shadowkind Quarter, through the city, to the citadel. And made us stand before Eldrion to face his wrath.

I remember the cruel curl of his lip as he looked down on my parents, the way his eyes glittered with malice. He wanted them to suffer. He wanted to make an example of them.

I have seen that look in his eyes so many times since, I truly believe that inflicting pain is at the core of his being. It is what he lives for. The thing that makes his heart beat faster and his blood run quicker.

My mother was first. Eldrion's guards held me in place, forcing me to watch as he tore the wings from her back with a force that ripped a sickening scream from her throat.

Her screams echoed off the stone walls of the citadel. I have remembered it for centuries. I still hear it in my sleep. But it's not her scream that ricochets around my mind when I am sleeping; it's my father's.

Watching her die broke him.

With a cruel smirk, Eldrion slit my mother's throat, letting her blood pour out onto the cold flagstones, filling the crevices between them, painting them scarlet as her entire body drained of colour and life.

I remember bracing myself to witness him do the same to my father.

But with him, Eldrion took his time, savouring each moment of agony. He shattered my father's limbs, the crack of bone mingling with his anguished sobs. Still crying for my mother.

In front of the watching crowd of traitors, who'd be summoned to observe their fate should they try again to rebel against him, Eldrion gouged out his eyes, condemning him to darkness before finally ending his life.

I was left kneeling in a pool of my parents' blood. But Eldrion wasn't done.

He had their broken bodies strung up on the city walls, and he took me as one of his slaves. A living trophy of his triumph.

I still remember the agony as they bound my wings, the feeling of my very essence being crushed and confined. The pain was excruciating, but it paled in comparison to the hatred that began to thicken around my heart.

Eldrion raised me as his pet, his jester, a source of amusement for his twisted court. Every day was a new humiliation, a fresh reminder of my powerlessness. But as I danced and tumbled for their entertainment, I nurtured the embers of rebellion in my soul.

I swore on my parents' memory that I would make Eldrion pay for what he did, that I would see his empire crumble and his life bleed out at my feet.

I vowed I would take back everything he stole from me, from all of us.

It's a vow I've carried with me every day since, through every indignity and abuse. It's the fire that has kept me going.

Biding my time.

Waiting.

Eldrion thinks he broke me, and that he moulded me into an obedient plaything. But he has no idea he has been nurturing a viper and keeping it in his nest.

Soon, very soon, he'll learn the true cost of his cruelty. And I'll be there to watch the light fade from his eyes, just as he watched the light fade from my mother's.

On that day, my vengeance will finally be complete. And the Shadowkind will rise from the ashes of Eldrion's tyranny with me as their leader.

All I need now is Alana and her power. She's the final piece in this game, my ultimate weapon.

Is there a part of me that feels sorry for her? Perhaps. But would she treat me any differently from Eldrion, given the chance?

No.

To every other fae in this land, Shadowkind are vermin.

Alana Leafborne is no different.

So, I'll use her and break her, just as I was used and broken.

In the end, she'll be nothing more than a stepping stone on my path to revenge and glory. A sad little footnote in the tale of my triumph.

For what are the feelings of one girl compared to the vengeance I've nursed for a lifetime? She's a small sacrifice to make for the greater goal.

I spot her across the clearing, a vision in a shimmering purple dress that clings to her curves. Even with the mask concealing her face, I know it's her, the empath Eldrion sent me to find.

I do not know why he wants her.

But I know why I need her.

She is my ticket to power and revenge.

I adjust my own red mask and saunter over, flashing her a charming smile. "Beautiful dress. Let me guess. Tonight, you will be changing into a peacock. Blues, purples, and golds. Strutting through the forest like a queen."

She tilts her head, intrigued. "A peacock? Is that what you think of me? A preening, strutting, princess?"

Her voice is like honey, and I let my eyes roam appreciatively over her body.

"We have not even had a conversation, and already you are insulting me? Does that usually work for you?"

I chuckle, moving closer, letting my energy brush against hers. "I'd have to spend more time with you in order to answer that question."

She smiles coyly, a blush colouring her cheeks. Perfect. I extend my hand. "May I ask your name?"

"Varia," she lies, placing her gloved hand in mine. I bring it to my lips, holding her gaze.

"It's a pleasure to meet you, Varia."

I can practically feel her curiosity and longing, even through the magical defences of her dress. This will be even easier than I thought. Eldrion's pet empath is so starved for genuine connection, for someone to truly see her, she's falling right into my hands.

Poor little bird. She has no idea she's flying straight into a trap, so desperate to spread her wings she can't see the bars of the cage closing around her.

But while Eldrion thinks he'll be the one to clip those lovely wings, he's wrong. I've spent decades as his slave, bowing and scraping, enduring humiliation and abuse, all the while plotting my revenge. And now, thanks to Alana, I finally have the means to get it.

Her magic will be the key that unlocks the door to Eldrion's downfall.

I break away from Alana with a wink. "I will seek your company later, when the dancing begins."

Weaving through the crowd, I watch her from the shadows, admiring the way the moonlight glints off her hair, the dreamy expression on her face as she thinks of me.

Eldrion can have his petty victories for now. Let him think his faithful dog is doing his bidding like a good little pup. He'll never see the dagger concealed behind my back until it is buried in his heart.

And as for Alana? I'll take such exquisite pleasure in making her fall desperately in love with me, all the while knowing it's nothing more than a means to an end.

There's a twisted thrill in deceiving something so pure.

An even bigger thrill in tricking someone who should be able to read my thoughts with a blink of her big, beautiful eyes.

By the time she realises it was all a lie, it will be too late. I'll have everything I need from her. And she'll be broken; a pretty little songbird with her heart carved out.

Such delicious cruelty. I can hardly wait to taste it.

But all in good time. For now, the dance is about to begin, and I have an empath to seduce.

I straighten my mask and stride back to Alana, bowing low and extending my hand in invitation.

Let the games begin.

TWO

Finn

OW

FROM HERE, SHE LOOKS LIKE AN ANGEL.

An angel of death. Standing beside her devil.

As she stares down at me from Eldrion's roof, I can feel the power radiating from her. She is glorious.

I always knew she was destined to shine like this, but I thought all I wanted was to capture her light, absorb it, crack the shards of brightness open and fill them with my darkness.

Now, I see it.

From here, I see her clearly for the first time, and I know I want her beside me for what's to come. I don't just want to use her and discard her; I want to draw out the twisted pieces of her soul that I've seen in the dark. The part of her that enjoyed binding me and taking me and showing

9

me the power that lives deep inside the basement of her being.

I want that part beside me when I take my revenge on Eldrion and his forsaken city.

I want to rule with Alana for the rest of eternity. Because the two of us together? When I am transformed and she is enlightened? We would be a force that could never be beaten.

"I'm coming to get you, Alana. Don't worry, I'm coming," I call up to her, and picture her eyes widening with relief. Because even though she is drawn to Eldrion, she loves me.

I made her love me.

I just didn't expect to love her back.

When I burst onto the roof, power and darkness surge through me like lightning through an onyx sky.

I know what I need to do.

It is so clear in my mind I can almost see it happening in front of me.

And there she is . . . Her glorious auburn hair loose over her shoulders, her body clearly naked beneath what looks like one of his robes.

She rushes towards me, almost smiling with relief, and I pull her into my arms. I motion for her to leave, to get to safety, and watch as Garratt shrugs at Eldrion. "Apologies, my lord. Business is business."

He starts to back away but Eldrion slams the door shut with a burst of power. "No one leaves!"

Alana turns to him, eyes flashing. For a fraction of a second, jealousy blooms in my gut; they share something. Something potent. I hadn't noticed it before but in this moment, I see it clearly.

It crackles in the air between them.

"What happened to 'you can leave if you want to'?" she hisses, talking to him the way lovers talk when they have enraged one another.

"I changed my mind," Eldrion growls. His eyes grow darker, and he flexes his fingers at his sides. Above him, the entire sky seems to darken too.

As Alana tugs against me, I make a feeble attempt to hold her back, then allow her to stride forward, magic flickering in her hands.

Now this . . . this is what I wanted to see.

Anticipation flickers deep in my core. Like this, she is magnificent. The power, the confidence, the way she strides towards him like she isn't even the smallest bit afraid of him. Like she knows she can conquer him with the click of her fingers if she wants to.

"I need him gone," she calls over her shoulder at me, hurling a ball of violet light towards Eldrion which he easily deflects.

"I don't want to fight you, Alana. But you have to see what he's doing. He's manipulating you." Eldrion keeps his gaze locked on Alana, but I know he wants to turn to me and show me the hate in his eyes.

He wants me dead. He sees me. But I see him too.

The only difference is, I have always seen behind his mask and he has only just learned to look through mine.

"Says you!" Alana yells, throwing another ball of light at him.

"Alana, don't trust him!" I call out. "Remember what he is and what his people have done. Remember all the things I showed you."

They circle each other. She flicks her wrist and, just like that, a dozen tiny icicles form in the air. She sends them hurtling towards him, but he bats them away.

"You should have done that last night," he taunts her, "before you decided to fuck me instead."

His words land like acid on my skin and, for a moment, I feel as if her icicles hit me instead of him.

I knew she'd fucked him in the tunnels, and I knew she'd fantasised about him. But hearing those words from his mouth, knowing she came here to kill him and he ended up inside her instead . . . That stings.

Alana hesitates and glances back at me. Her lips quiver, as if she's about to tell me she's sorry and ask for my forgiveness.

In that moment, Eldrion hurls a vortex of shadow at her. She ducks beneath it and retaliates with her own purple smoke-like shadows that creep towards Eldrion.

I have never seen anything like it, and I have no idea how she is creating them. But as her power shimmers on her skin and flickers in her eyes, my jealousy fades.

She is doing this for me.

I made her like this.

She is mine, and he will not take her — or my victory — from me.

"I might not be able to kill you," she says coldly, "but I have no problem taking your powers from you."

My upper lip curls into a slow, delicious grin. Yes, Alana. Take his powers. Take them for me.

Her smoke winds up Eldrion's body as he fights back with all his might, his wings flaring out, roaring with fury. The shadows pulse with dark energy but Alana's smoke keeps pulling, draining away his magic bit by bit. He's weakening, I can sense it.

Eldrion does not fight back. Is he hoping she'll change her mind? Or is he completely naive to how powerful she really is?

When she doesn't stop, he gathers his shadows and hurls them towards her with a roar. "Don't make me hurt you, Alana!"

And this is it.

This is everything I need.

The stars and planets have aligned.

I have my chance.

Without hesitation, I leap in front of Alana, spreading my wings wide, and take the full force of Eldrion's attack. His shadow magic slams into my chest, sending me flying into the wall. I crumple to the ground as pain ricochets through my body. My eyes roll back, darkness descends, and I allow the pain to engulf me.

Everything is dark.

Pitch dark.

I am everywhere and nowhere at the same time. My body is riddled with pain but also feels lighter than it ever has before.

"I can't leave him." I hear Alana's voice – a whisper that soothes and tantalises me. As it settles into the deep crevices of my body, it turns into something else.

A flicker. A crackling sensation, like embers and ashes warming the inside of my bones.

Slowly, the embers grow hotter. Flames of pain flicker to life and lick the spaces between my ribs. The sensation spreads outward, flowing through my veins, smouldering on the surface of my skin.

When it reaches my wings, I try to move but I can't.

I feel them twitch and simmer, like slivers of tree bark being held over a fire. They curl and crackle.

It is happening.

They are changing.

I am changing.

As Alana holds me, I feel Eldrion's shadows, his magic, flowing into me. It worked. I have what I need from him now. I have what I needed from her.

Her warmth disappears. I hear her turning on Eldrion, I feel her magic flickering in the air around me.

I open my mouth to call for her, but her name turns to a sharp, disarming gasp of air, swelling in my lungs, burning my throat. Something shifts beneath me. The sensation of solid ground slipping away from me is overwhelming. I try to beat my wings, but I can't move them. I try to call her name again, but it does not come.

When my eyes finally flutter open, I realise I am floating. Rising.

I find Alana and watch her stagger back in shock as my body contorts and breaks and reshapes itself. I scream in agony, but as the sound bleeds into the air, it becomes not pain but triumph.

I am being reborn.

I am becoming what I was always meant to be; the creature that has been locked inside me for centuries.

A rush of pure, unadulterated power surges through me. I splay my arms, and my wings. They are black now, and large enough to block out the sun. And I know, hovering above Eldrion's castle, that nothing can touch me now.

I am the most powerful creature in the entire land.

And I will have my vengeance.

I watch as Eldrion tries to summon his precious shadows back to him, but they no longer obey his commands.

They are mine.

"They do not listen to you now, Eldrion," I hiss. "They listen to me."

I barely even need to think about what I want them to do

to him; it is like they are me. They are inside my head. My body. My mind. My soul.

They are mine.

And they have Eldrion trapped.

With viperous strength, they coil around the fae lord, trapping him. Pinning him. Binding him with their darkness.

I focus my gaze on Alana. "Thank you," I tell her. "I could not have done this without you." I extend my hand.

She stares at me in dawning horror as she realises the truth. That I used her. That this was my plan.

"I want you beside me when I take the world back to how it was before."

Alana clutches her stomach. She shakes her head, her eyes growing damp with tears. Beside her, Briony is sobbing and trembling.

Weak. They are all so weak.

A sigh racks my chest. I really did think Alana might be better than this. Still, there is time for me to show her the error of her ways.

"Poor sweet girl." I laugh as she vomits on the floor. "I guess this means you won't be joining me after all?"

Alana rips her gaze away from me and blasts my shadows with her magic, begging Eldrion to help her.

He tumbles free, but it's too late.

I rise higher into the air, my wings filling the sky, shadows swirling around me. I breathe them in, let them swell in my lungs and fill the dark void in my ribcage, and then I am gone.

Do they think it's over?

Do they think this is it?

Sad, pathetic creatures.

I finally have the power I need. And I will use it to take everything I deserve.

THREE

Alana

_____

 ain swarms behind my eyes, needling at me like wasps. Blurring my vision. Although I'm still wearing Eldrion's robe, I feel suddenly exposed. Completely bare. As if my body and soul have been ripped from my bones and laid out on the floor for everyone to see. Bloody and shapeless.

Finn was dead.

And then he wasn't.

And now he's a monster.

I stare at the empty space where, just moments ago, he hovered in the air in front of us. My mind is reeling, trying to process what happened.

Every time I blink, I see him behind my eyes.

His once playful, mischievous features twisted into something dark and sinister. His eyes, usually a warm, inviting blue, glowing a deep, malevolent red.

When he turned them on me, it was as if he could see into the depths of my soul. As if he could see every deep, dark thought I'd ever had and was determined to coax them to the surface.

His skin, previously smooth and unblemished, became covered in intricate, swirling tattoos that looked like living shadows. They snaked up his arms, across his chest, and up the sides of his face, pulsing and undulating as if they were trying to both consume him and free him.

But it's not his eyes or his skin that has lodged in my brain.

It is his wings.

No longer small or delicate. No longer a part of him that I could bind or play with.

They became huge, larger than Eldrion's, stretching out like the wings of a fallen angel. Instead of their dull, muted shade, they became pitch black. They seemed to absorb the light around them, pulling in the shadows until Finn was cloaked in an aura of darkness.

As he moved, the shadows danced around him, swirling and shifting like a living entity. They caressed his skin, wrapped around his limbs, as if they were an extension of him.

When he turned his red-eyed gaze on me, his lips curling into a cruel, mocking smile, I realised the Finn I had known was gone. Or perhaps that he never existed.

In his place was a monster; a being of pure darkness.

And I have no one to blame but myself for what will happen next.

Something touches my arm. I jolt away from the sensation, purple light crackling in my palms. When I realise it's Briony, I freeze but do not lower my hands.

She shakes her head and holds up her palms. "Alana, it's me."

"And it was Finn," I whisper, looking out over the awakening citadel. Golden hues dancing on the rooftops. The day is slowly beginning, just like any other, except nothing will ever be as it was before, and Finn's storm clouds still paint dark bruises in the sky above us.

Wiping tears from her face, Briony nods at me. "I know," she says. "It was Finn. He . . ." A violent sob escapes her lips and she falls forward into my embrace. I hold her as if I'm her mother and she's my child. Usually, it is her comforting me. But now, she feels small and fragile, and I am too numb to feel anything at all.

Her wings twitch. I stare at them. Pale grey, almost translucent.

The way Finn's were.

Is that why I underestimated him? Because I saw what he wasn't instead of what he was?

The rooftop is eerily silent now, the only sound being the distant rumble of thunder and Eldrion breathing raggedly beside me.

My heart hammers in my chest, a sickening mix of fear, confusion, and dawning horror swirling inside me.

Finn, my Finn, the one who was the one steady thing amongst all the turmoil of the past few months . . . He is gone.

And it was all because of me.

I clutch my stomach, doubling over as another wave of nausea hits me.

I am no longer numb.

I am broken.

I can't breathe, can't think. The image of Finn's red eyes, his shadowy tattoos, his twisted limbs reshaping themselves into something monstrous – it's seared into my mind. Worse than the visions that have haunted me because they are real and I cannot undo them or forget them.

"What have I done?" I whisper, my voice cracking. "What have I unleashed?"

Beside me, Eldrion staggers to his feet, his face pale and his eyes wide with shock. He looks down at his hands, flexing his fingers. His gaze darkens. He splays his wings and draws himself up to his fullest height.

My breath hitches in my chest. I wait for the shadows to come to him, but nothing happens. Everything is completely still.

"My powers," he murmurs, his jaw twitching. "He's taken my powers."

"What do you mean, he's taken your powers?" I stride forward and grip his wrist, staring at his hand as if I might be able to coax them back to him. "How is that possible? He had no magic. The Shadowkind have no magic." I look at Briony as if she might have an answer, but she just buries her face in her hands and takes a long, shuddering breath.

Still flexing his wings, Eldrion shakes his head, his expression grave. "The shadows, the darkness . . . they don't respond to me anymore. I don't know how he did it, but he took them."

A violent chill drags through my body, making it shiver.

"The demon I saw . . ." I am still holding Eldrion's wrist. His skin is cold beneath my touch.

He meets my eyes and nods solemnly. "Finn . . . it was him all along."

"But there were more." I pace away from him, pinching the bridge of my nose, trying to both remember and forget the visions I saw. "There were so many more."

When I turn around, Eldrion is staring at Briony. "The Shadowkind," he mutters. Now he is pacing. His wings twitch but they seem, somehow, even though they are barely moving, to have lost some of their strength.

In one stride, Eldrion has closed the distance between him and Briony and is holding her tight by her shoulders. Her eyes widen, and her dark hair falls forward into her face as he shakes her a little.

"Is that what he's planning?" he hisses.

Briony opens her mouth but can't seem to form any words.

"Is it?" Eldrion's grip is tightening on her shoulders. She winces and tries to pull away but he doesn't let her.

"I don't know what you mean," she says meekly.

"Is he planning to turn all of you?" Eldrion barks the question, his face inches away from hers.

Briony frowns and stutters as she speaks. "No. No. He planned to kill you. I know that. He wanted Alana to help. He wanted to take over the city. But he never said anything about . . ." She trails off, unable to finish her sentence.

"About turning into a demon," I mutter.

Eldrion releases a low growl and lets her go. I can see thoughts flitting across his face, but he doesn't vocalise them.

"We have to stop him," I say, forcing myself to stand up straight despite the trembling in my legs. "Whatever he's planning next, we have to stop him. We have to get your magic back and stop him."

Eldrion looks at me, his eyes filled with a mix of emotions I can't quite read. Anger, fear, regret . . . and something else, something deeper that I can't put a name to.

"Alana," he says, taking a step towards me. "I . . ."

But before he can finish, Briony interrupts, clearing her throat as she steels herself to speak. "Maybe we should get inside." She looks at the sky as if Finn might reappear at any moment. "We all betrayed Finn in one way or another." She looks at me, then wrings her hands together. "And he doesn't forget things like that easily. He'll be back for us. Won't he? I mean, he's not just going to let us go after all that?"

I nod, tearing my gaze away from Eldrion. She's right. We can't stay out here. And I can't think about what happens next while I'm standing here, naked beneath Eldrion's robe, the feel of him still on my skin and the scent of him dizzying my head.

I take a deep breath, trying to steady myself.

How could I have trusted Finn? How could I not see what he was?

How could I have ever believed I loved him?

I STAND IN ELDRION'S CHAMBER, HASTILY PULLING ON A pair of leather breeches and a dark tunic, provided by Briony before she hastily backed out of the room and left us alone.

My hands are shaking, making the simple task of dressing myself more difficult than it should be. Behind me, I can feel Eldrion's eyes on my back, watching my every move.

"Stop staring," I snap, whirling around to face him as I button up the tunic. "And pay attention to what I'm saying. What was that? You're the all-knowing, all-powerful Lord of Luminael. You didn't see that coming? You didn't know your powers could be stolen that way?"

"No more than you knew you were being used as a pawn in his plan to steal them from me." Eldrion rises from his armchair and paces to the window.

"You're still staring." I pull the tunic closed over my breasts and finish fastening it.

He scoffs, folding his arms across his chest. "It's hard to focus when you're putting on such a show."

I glare at him, my cheeks burning with a mix of anger and hatred. "I would never put on a show for you," I retort, jaw twitching with fury.

"Yes, you would." He strides towards me.

Our eyes meet. My skin warms, fizzes, tingles with heat. How does he do this to me? It's like every emotion – fear, anger, sadness – bubbles to the surface of my skin, and multiplies, and swells, and turns into undeniable, painfully loud, screaming thunderbolts of arousal instead.

As if he is the only thing that will soothe the way I feel.

And yet also the only thing to ignite it.

"I despise you for what you have done," I whisper. "What you did to the Shadowkind. What you did to Kayan. What you did to me. Don't think that because we have a common cause now, we are friends."

Eldrion's jaw clenches, his eyes hardening. "What did I do to you, Alana?"

I stare at him for a long moment, then whisper, "You made me want you even though I hate you."

He slams a heavy hand onto my waist and tugs me towards him. "I could say the same thing to you," he growls.

I can't stop looking at his lips. I want to melt into him. I want his hands, and fingernails, and teeth on my skin. I want him to destroy me so I can no longer feel anything except him.

"Finn is more powerful than you now." I meet his eyes.

"You think I don't know that? I can feel the emptiness where my powers used to be." He is still holding on to my waist. "You're an empath, Alana. How the fuck could you not see it?"

"Don't you dare put this on me," I retort, caught between feeling utterly distraught and utterly furious. "You're the one who started this, Eldrion. You brought me here. You put me in Finn's way. You caused this, not me."

I don't believe what I'm saying, but perhaps Eldrion does because his eyes flash with anger, and for a moment, I think he might actually strike me.

Instead, he grabs my face roughly, his fingers digging into my cheeks. I can feel the heat of his breath on my lips as he leans in, so close that I can count the flecks of gold in his stormy grey eyes. There's a hunger there, a raw intensity that matches my own, and before I can protest, his mouth crashes down on mine.

The kiss is brutal, all teeth and tongues and pent-up frustration. Eldrion's grip on me tightens, bruising and possessive, as if he's trying to brand me as his own. But I refuse to submit easily, teeth nipping at his lower lip in defiance.

In a frenzy, he rips my clothes off and we stumble towards the armchair.

My nails rake down his back, leaving angry red marks beneath his wings, but Eldrion only growls in response, then spins me around and pushes me down so I'm kneeling in the chair, leaning over the back, waiting for him to enter me.

When he does, he slams into me so hard the chair nearly topples over. I brace a hand on the wall to steady us. He hooks one arm around my waist and furiously circles my already swollen clit. There is no warm-up, no slow building of pleasure. It hits me like a tsunami and is almost painful in its intensity.

It is so much, I can barely make a sound.

I bite my lip, grip the chair and the wall, push back onto him again and again and again.

He calls my name. Utters it like a curse word. Like he hates me, and hates how much he wants me, and this is his vengeance.

This exquisite torture is how he will end me.

With waves of pleasure that blind me to anything but him.

His thrusts are a promise that he will not stop until I am drowning in him, and only him. Until he has dragged me down to the depths of my own desire and abandoned me there, unable to breathe, tethered to his darkness.

When he comes, the sound of his release drives me over the precipice of my own orgasm.

I shudder and quake beneath him, my body turning to nothing but a blazing pool of skin and flesh and bone.

I expect him to pull away from me quickly and leave me quivering and shaking and cold without his presence. But he stays, arm curled around me, holding me as I tremble.

When I start to cry, he bites my shoulder. But it is tender. And the tenderness makes me cry harder. "I hate you," I sob.

"I know." The bite turns to a kiss.

He lets me cry.

And then he's gone. I feel him move away from me, hear him dressing. I sink down into the chair, turn around, then rise to my feet.

When I'm dressed too, and we're staring at each other in

silence, I realise – perhaps for the first time – that he is not as beautiful as I thought he was.

He is flawed.

In all ways.

And for a terrifying moment the hate in my heart becomes softer around its edges.

Eldrion frowns at me, then runs a hand through his hair, his brow furrowed. "Whatever Finn has become, he's dangerous. And he's angry. At both of us."

"Not just us." I roll up my sleeves, then pick up the boots Briony gave me and pull them onto my feet. "He is furious with every Sunborne fae in the city. Furious with Luminael itself."

"So what's his next move?" Eldrion asks, pacing the room. This time, when he looks at me, it's as if we are equals and he genuinely needs to know my answer.

"I don't know. But—" a violent shock of pain hits me between the eyes and I stumble backwards. Bright light fills my vision, blinding me, then solidifying into something else.

The forest.

The campfire, the leaves, the canopy above. But it is darkening. Smoke curls around the trees. No, not smoke – shadows.

Then, in the darkness . . . red, blinking eyes. Black wings. Screams, shadows, wings.

"Alana!" Eldrion's voice shakes me back to reality. His hands are on my shoulders, gripping me tightly, and he's staring with wide, worried eyes. "What did you see?" he barks.

"We have to warn the others." I can barely speak. Fear has its clammy hand over my mouth, pressing the words back down into my throat.

"Others?"

"Finn. He's going to kill them."

"Who?" Eldrion steps back from me, frowning.

"The Shadowkind and the Leafborne. I saw him. In the forest with them . . ." I hesitate but force myself to trust Eldrion. Because, right now, I have no other choice. "They're hiding in the forest north of the city. Behind a shield. But Finn can get past it. They'll let him back in, and he'll—"

Eldrion nods slowly and steeples his fingers together. "We might be too late," he says gravely. "But we'll try."

FOUR

Finn
_____

I materialise on the edge of the forest. From here, the ancient oak trees stretch up towards the brightening sky like sentinels guarding old and precious secrets.

Behind me, the sky above Eldrion's castle is still dark. Here, it is pale blue, kissed with delicate white clouds.

How deceptive. How ironic.

Calling to me from deep inside the forest, I can feel the energy of the Leafborne and the Shadowkind. I sense them. It swells from beneath the canopy, and makes me wonder how no one found us while we were here.

I pass through the shield with ease, sighing with pleasure as I draw closer to the camp.

As I move, the shadows move with me. They did not do this for Eldrion. They did not bind themselves to his form and shift with him as he walked. For me, they do.

Because they were always meant to be mine.

Just like Alana was always meant to be mine.

I raise my arm and turn it over, examining the inky, smoke-like tattoos that now decorate my skin. As a beam of sunlight breaks through the canopy and illuminates my pale skin, I realise my veins too are becoming darker.

Like my soul, and my wings, and my destiny.

My feet are bare, my chest too. But I do not feel cold. I feel warm, as if a furnace is burning in my gut.

With each footstep, the foliage around me seems to darken, and shrivel, and wilt. It recoils from me the way Alana did.

But it will return, and so will she.

When I show her how powerful I am, and that being by my side is the sensible choice, she will crumble like ash in the wind.

Approaching the campsite, I notice the crackle of the fire and the scent of the smoke. My senses are heightened. I hear the movement of wings and feet, and the low chatter of voices.

I am drawing closer to the clearing when I hear a familiar voice. "Finn?"

I turn to see Raine, the pregnant Leafborne who hates me with a passion that almost rivals Eldrion's. She thinks she has hidden it, but I've always seen it there. In her eyes. Congealing like ink on water.

She immediately brings a hand to her stomach, assessing me.

I smile at her, and feel my eyes flashing red.

My wings quiver and slowly unfurl.

Raine steps backwards. She meets the trunk of a large oak tree and presses herself against it. She raises a hand, bringing green flashes of earth magic into her palm. "I always knew—"

Before she can finish her pathetic attempt to wound me with her words or her woefully inadequate powers, I give a flick of my wrist and the shadows that live in the darkness behind the trees are unleashed.

They engulf her in seconds, and she falls to the ground.

She's still breathing, but barely.

She will be gone soon.

And the baby? I pause and try to decide whether I care.

I do not.

Before walking away, I crouch down and tilt my head so I can look into her wide, terrified eyes. "You should know," I whisper, lowering my lips to her ear, "that by the time the sun reaches its peak today, the Leafborne will be extinct. There will be only one of you remaining. And she was never really one of you. She was always better than your kind."

Raine's lips part and she coughs. "Alana," she splutters.

I stroke her hair from her face, then pinch her jaw between my thumb and forefinger. "Yes," I whisper soothingly. "Alana. She is the best of you, and the worst of you. And she will rule by my side."

Another cough. Blood this time, trickling from the corner of her mouth.

I frown and stand up, then I splay my arms and begin to inhale. I breathe the shadows deep into my lungs. I let them fill me up. I hold them inside me. And then I release a deep, earth-shattering roar and set them free.

They fly through the forest, weaving between the trees. Over and under and around. They block out the freckles of light that filter through the canopy. Everything darkens.

The air grows cold and heavy, a thick black fog rolling in at my bidding.

The first scream that pierces the air is the most delicious sound I have ever heard. I close my eyes and relish it. There is another, and another.

They start to run, but the shadows are herding them for me. Tying them in knots, confusing them, gathering them exactly where I need them.

I release a low, gut-trembling sigh.

Their fear feels so good. It feeds the darkness inside me, yet makes me hungry for more.

When I reach the campsite, I watch from the shadows as the Leafborne fae huddle together, their delicate wings trembling with fear.

My shadows have encircled them, pinned them together.

They think they chose this to protect themselves but the shadows drove them to it.

On the opposite side of the camp, the Shadowkind do the same.

They do not know that no harm will come to them today.

I emerge from the darkness and move towards the fire. Although it is still daylight beyond the forest, here it might as well be the middle of the night.

The Leafborne try to huddle closer, move farther away.

One or two throw their magic towards me, but the shadows simply swallow it.

When I left here, I was pathetic. Small, weak, unable to fight.

Now, I am bigger than them, more powerful than them. And I am the fight.

As they blink at me from their huddle of bodies, I savour their terror, letting it wash over me like a dark elixir.

With only a thought, I send long tendrils of inky blackness snaking towards the Leafborne. The shadows creep in from the edges of the clearing, cutting off every escape route, every path to safety.

The fae scream, their voices high and thin with terror as they separate and try to flee. But there is nowhere to go, nowhere to hide. My shadows are everywhere.

One of them, a young male with gossamer wings the colour of spring leaves, steps forward, his hands raised in a futile attempt at defence. He summons his own magic, a glimmering shield of emerald light that pulses and shimmers in the darkness.

But it's no use. My shadows simply flow around his magic, engulfing him in a writhing mass of darkness. He screams, his voice choked into a gurgling cry as my magic tears at his flesh, ripping and shredding until there is nothing left but a broken, lifeless husk on the floor.

Power is thrumming through my veins, intoxicating and addictive.

"Run, little Leafbornes," I purr. "Run, and let the shadows feast upon your fear."

The fae scatter, their screams ringing out through the forest as my shadows pursue them, relentless and inexorable. They tear through the forest, fleeing from me in blind panic.

But there is no escape, and there is no refuge from the darkness that has come to claim them. One by one, they fall, their light extinguished forever as my shadows consume them whole.

And it feels . . . so hellishly good.

With every heart that stops beating, my power seems to surge.

With every scream, and vibration of fear, my wings grow stronger.

With every death, I live louder.

I turn to face the Shadowkind. They have been spared, and they are huddled together, their eyes wide.

I can feel their uncertainty, their confusion, but also their curiosity. They know something momentous is happening, something that will change the course of their lives forever.

I step forward, my wings unfurling behind me like a cloak of purest, darkest night. The shadows dance around me, caressing my skin, whispering their dark secrets in my ears. I feel their power, and the intoxicating rush of knowing I hold the fate of an entire kingdom in my hands.

"Shadowkind," I say, my voice echoing through the clearing like a thunderclap. "Your new destiny is upon you. As the first of our kind to believe in me, and follow me into the forest when we fled from Eldrion's cruelty, you will be the first to reap the benefits of my transformation."

I spot Yarrow. He is the only one who looks intrigued rather than afraid.

"The time has come for you to take your rightful place in this world." I focus my gaze on him; my oldest friend. "The time has come to rise up and undo the wrongs that were done to us for so many centuries."

I can see the hesitation in their eyes, the fear that holds them back. But I know that deep down, they yearn for this, for the chance to be something. To be what they were always meant to be. I just need to unlock it for them.

"I'm going to offer you a choice," I continue, my gaze sweeping over them. "Join me, and be a part of the new world order that I will create. A world where Shadowkind are no longer the outcasts, the pariahs, but the rulers and the conquerors. Where we embrace the power that has been dormant inside us for centuries."

I pause, allowing my words to settle in the air around us.

"And if we don't join you?" a meek voice drifts up from one of the younger fae at the front of the crowd. "What if we just want to get away from here and live a peaceful life?"

A few of the others murmur in agreement.

I cannot have that.

"Well, then you can refuse, of course." I stop speaking, allowing the silence that swells between the trees to be broken only by the distant screams of the dying Leafborne. I lower my wings, allowing them a full view of the carnage that lies behind me.

I allow my shadows to curl upwards, dancing around my limbs.

My eyes flash red.

I fix them on the one who spoke up.

"Who will be the first to join me?"

FIVE

Garratt

_____

"*O*ut of the way!" I push through the crowd waiting to be let into the inn, and unlock the door.

"What got your mudweed in a stew this morning, Garratt?" someone calls with a chuckle.

"I think he had a late night," says another. "Never thought you had the charm to woo two females at the same time."

I grab hold of Elodie's arm and heave her through the door after me. Pria slams it closed and bolts it shut, then turns and folds her arms in front of her chest. She taps her foot as if she's annoyed I didn't correct the hecklers' assumption.

Or maybe she's annoyed I never tried to get into her bed.

Who the fuck knows.

Right now, we've got bigger things to worry about.

Elodie tugs against my grip and I realise I'm still holding on to her. Tight.

Shaking her off, like a piece of garbage stuck to my shoe, I hurry over to the bar, slam three glasses down on the counter, and pour three almost-overflowing whiskies.

I down mine, refill it, and down it again before offering Pria and Elodie theirs.

I can hardly breathe. I'm not as fit as I used to be, but it's not the journey from the castle to the inn that has winded me; it's the hammering drumbeat of fear in my chest.

It is so loud, so hard, so fierce I can hardly breathe.

I lean forward onto my forearms and close my eyes.

Outside, regulars are still banging on the door demanding I open up – now more annoyed than amused by my strange entrance.

Elodie hugs her waist. She hasn't taken even a sip of her whisky. Pria, however, is drinking hers slowly, and studying me as if she's waiting for me to say something profound.

Panic is rising like bile from my gut to my throat.

I tug at my collar and turn away from them, leaning back on the bar, trying desperately to remember how to breathe.

"Garratt?" Elodie's voice is willowy and small and makes me want to throw her out into the street with the others. Except then I think about actually doing that, and it makes me want to do the opposite: pull her close and hold her there.

I reach for the whisky bottle again, hand shaking, and this time don't bother pouring it into the glass. I just take a deep swig and wipe my mouth with the back of my hand.

"Shit." I shake my head and force myself to turn back to face them.

"Garratt! Open up!" A fist on the door. It makes me jump and sends shivers of fear skittering down my spine.

I see his eyes. I see his wings. I feel the shift in the air. Not just the air. The universe. The cosmos.

In that moment, as Finn rose into the air and his wings became thick, black harbingers of death, I knew this was what I'd always feared.

Even though I didn't realise it.

The catastrophe our ancestors talked about, and the secrets they kept guarded in the library, and the centuries they spent trying to carefully manage the peace of our kingdom . . . This is it.

This is the moment that was always coming and yet never foretold.

Not out loud.

Because if it had been . . . I would never have . . .

I lose my grasp on the whisky bottle and it falls to the floor. It splinters into several thick shards, and the smell of alcohol fills the air.

"Garratt! If you don't open the door we'll come in through the bloody window! What are you playing at?" More fists, more noise.

I am staring at the whisky, watching it soak into the cracks between the tiles.

The edges of my vision have blurred. I can't think straight. I have never felt fear before. Not like this.

Perhaps I have.

When I looked into my wife's face when she told me she was expecting a baby, and when she got sick, and when she died, and when the baby died with her, and I was left alone.

I drop to the floor.

I can't breathe. I can't see. I can't breathe.

"For fuck's sake, Elodie, help him," Pria barks.

In the periphery of my blurred vision, I see Pria march over to the door and fling it open. A shaft of light strikes across the dark flagstone floor. I shield my eyes. I still can't breathe. I am on the floor in front of the bar, knees drawn up to my chest, behaving like a terrified child, and I can't do anything to snap myself out of it because all I can see is the eyes.

The red, blinking eyes of the demon that will destroy us all.

"Fuck off!" Pria yells at the customers who are waiting to be let in.

"You can't tell us to fuck off, this isn't your place—" someone starts to argue with her.

She slams her foot into the floor and flashes her guard's badge. "Lord Eldrion has ordered this place to be shut down. If the courtyard isn't clear by the time he gets here, I don't want to know what happens next. Do you?"

There's a simmering pause. They know she's lying, but the threat of Eldrion is still enough to make them scurry away silently, lips pressed tightly together, thoughts locked inside instead of spoken aloud.

Elodie kneels in front of me and puts her hands on my shoulders. "Garratt . . . are you all right?" she asks.

I try to focus on her face. She is pale, and her complexion is clammy. She looks terrified. But clearly she doesn't feel it. Not the way I do.

"Of course, he's not all right." Pria tuts and strides over to the bar. She walks behind it, rummages, then returns with a paper bag full of peanuts. She empties it onto the floor, then shoves the bag into my hand. "Breathe into this. Slowly."

"Can I have one?" Elodie asks, pressing her palm to her chest.

Pria rolls her eyes. "No."

I start to breathe. Slowly. Counting. Pria presses a firm hand to mine and meets my eyes, nodding and breathing along with me.

We stay like this for what feels like hours but is likely only minutes.

When I can finally breathe again, I lower the bag into my lap and nod at Pria. "Thank you."

She shrugs and sits down on the floor next to me, avoiding the whisky spill. Elodie sits down too, crossing her legs.

"So," Pria says, "are you good?"

I fold my arms in front of my stomach. "I'm all right."

"Good," she replies. "Because that's the one chance you get to freak out. Do that again, I'll kill you myself."

The look in her eyes tells me she's deadly serious.

"Why would you——" Elodie mutters, frowning at Pria as if she can't understand what's happening.

"Because all hell is about to break loose, and if we're going to get out of this city before it does, we need to work together." Pria looks at me. "Right?"

"Right." I stagger to my feet. "In which case, we're going to need more whisky."

I STUMBLE BEHIND THE BAR AND GRAB ANOTHER BOTTLE, MY hands still shaking. I pour two more glasses and slide them across the counter to Pria and Elodie.

"What the fuck . . ." I mutter, taking a long gulp of the amber liquid. It burns my throat but does fuck all to calm my nerves. "Okay, okay." I'm shaking with adrenaline now, but at least I can see straight. "Okay. So . . ." I inhale deeply. "So, what the fuck was that?"

Pria downs her whisky in one swift motion. "A demon," she says flatly. "Or something close to it. I've heard stories, whispers, but I never thought . . ." She shakes her head, her pale wings twitching.

"Stories?" I grip my glass a little tighter. "What kind of stories?"

For the first time in the years I've known her, a look of vulnerability flashes across Pria's face. "My grandfather told me the Shadowkind used to be stronger," she says tightly. "He never explained what he meant. He started to. He was old, and sick, and my grandmother stopped him, but I always wondered what he meant."

"Stronger?" I put my glass down on the bar and nod slowly, trying to shake the pieces into place. "All of you? Not just Finn?"

Taking a swig directly from the bottle because her glass is empty, Pria says, "Maybe. Yes. I don't know. My grandfather said we used to be stronger and then they bound us. That's why they bound us. To stop us becoming our true selves." She pauses, brow pinched into a tight frown. "I had no idea what he meant. But maybe this is what he meant."

Elodie is staring into her glass, her face pale. "So there could be more?" She looks from me to Pria. "What are we going to do?" she whispers.

I run a hand through my hair, my mind racing. "We have to get out of here. Now. Before he comes for us." The thought sends a fresh wave of terror through me.

"Why would he come for us?" Elodie asks. "We're not important. We didn't do anything to him."

"I was playing him and Eldrion against one another!" I shout at her, and watch as she blinks under the weight of my rage. "If he finds out, you don't think he'll want revenge?"

Pria scoffs. "You think that's our biggest problem? Finn's not just going to come for you, Garratt. He's going to destroy this whole fucking city. You heard him. You saw him. He's got bigger plans than taking revenge on an elf who stabbed him in the back."

Her words hit me like a punch to the gut. She's right. This is bigger than just me. Why would Finn care about me?

I'm nothing. A speck on the landscape of whatever he has in store for this city.

So, the question is, do I care what happens to anyone else?

Do I stick around and warn the other elves what's coming their way? Or do I save myself?

SIX

Alana

*E*ldrion summons two guards and orders them to prepare horses for us. He is different somehow, and yet it is not a physical difference. It's in the way the air moves around him, and the timbre of his voice.

Unnoticeable, perhaps, to anyone but me.

Studying him as he throws himself up onto the back of a large white stallion, I let down the gates in my mind and reach for him. In the past, it hasn't worked. But something tells me that now, it might.

Next to me, Briony watches as if she knows I am attempting something I shouldn't be.

At first, an overwhelming sense of adrenaline washes over me. It settles on my skin, burning with its intensity.

I try to move past it and see what lies beneath. But it hardens and solidifies in front of me.

"I might have lost my shadow magic," Eldrion says, staring

down at me from his horse, "but my mind magic is intact, Alana. You can't read me. You never could."

I press my lips together and swallow forcefully. How did he know? Did he feel me reaching into his mind?

"What about your other magic?" I ask, choosing not to defend myself but to, instead, jump up onto my own horse's back and take hold of her reins, waiting for Briony to climb up behind me and loop her arms around my waist.

Eldrion shakes his head. "Everything else I possessed was powered by the shadows." He looks up at the sky, dark and brooding, thunderclouds gathered above the castle as if they are preparing to unleash the most almighty storm on us. "And now the shadows belong to Finn."

"And you don't think we can get them back?" I ask him.

"We?"

"You."

"Maybe." He takes hold of his horse's reins. "But I doubt it's something I could do without your assistance."

I let that idea settle in my head for a moment. Eldrion can only get his magic back if I help him? Why would I do that? Why would I give him back the power that allowed him to be so cruel for so long?

"Shadowkind . . ." I mutter, stroking my horse's mane. I glance back at Briony, but she lowers her head as if she doesn't want to confront what I'm thinking.

When I turn my head to meet Eldrion's eyes, I realise they are the same as mine: scared, ashamed, but also determined. "I suppose it makes sense. Perhaps this is what they used to be. Perhaps this is why their wings were bound?"

Eldrion nods slowly. "Perhaps."

I pinch the bridge of my nose and try to centre my thoughts. "How did you not know? You are the oldest fae in the kingdom, Eldrion. How did you not know what he was?"

Eldrion rests one hand on his horse's neck and bites the inside of his cheek. After staring at me for a moment, he laughs. The sound surprises me. He shakes his head and laughs again. "Don't you see, Alana?"

A shudder grips my shoulders and forces me to hunch forward a little, as if the movement might shrug off whatever haunts me.

"My visions were meaningless. All this time, I was exactly as weak as my parents and my brother always told me I was. I did not see what Finn was. I misread every sign that was sent to me. I failed."

He speaks without an ounce of self-pity in his voice, and yet the rawness of his words takes me by complete surprise.

I want to tell him he didn't fail, and that his parents were wrong about him, but I have no idea why I feel the need to offer him comfort.

So, instead, I remain silent.

Eldrion watches me for a moment. Then turns his gaze forward. "We are wasting time." He clicks his tongue and taps the horse's flank. "To the woods," he commands.

I wait a beat, then follow him, Briony holding on tightly behind me.

Should I be following him?

Have I simply stopped believing in one monster and turned to another instead?

THE CASTLE LOOMS BEHIND US, SILHOUETTED AGAINST THE dark thunderous sky. I can't help looking back at it. Once a prison, it now feels strangely like a sanctuary. And the desire to lock myself away there, away from all of this, is almost too much to ignore.

Eldrion, however, keeps his gaze fixed ahead. We leave the citadel, enter the city, and follow the same path we took the night he made me accompany him to the inn.

When we pass through the streets, they are eerily quiet. I have no idea if the inhabitants of Luminael saw what happened above the castle. Did they see Finn's transformation? The shadows swirling in the sky? Did they feel something shift in the air?

They must have, because there are barely any signs of life.

"It's eerie," Briony whispers. "I don't like it. Where is everyone?"

Windows are shuttered, market stalls are vacant, and there is an unsettling lack of noise. No chatter or movements of the day beginning.

I glance at Eldrion. I might not be able to read his emotions, but my powers are still intact. So, I let the gates down and reach behind the closed doors as we pass them.

It is probably a foolish decision. I am weak, and my own emotions are running so high I can barely contain them. But I need to take back some control. I need to do something to make me feel as if I have a grasp on what's happening around us.

The first thing I feel is silence. It is almost deafening in its intensity. A swirling cyclone of silence. Like shadows. But then the silence is ripped apart, and it is swallowed by fear.

My eyes blur. I grip on to my horse with my thighs. I hold the reins tighter. My stomach twists with the overwhelming sense of terror that swells inside the houses and taverns of Luminael.

They saw.

And they are afraid.

When I slam the gates back down and look at Eldrion, he has slowed his pace and is staring at me. My skin is clammy, and I know my cheeks are flushed. My hair sticks to the side of my face. I push it back and try to remember how to breathe.

"They know," I mutter.

Eldrion nods slowly. "Of course they know, Alana. Even if they hadn't seen it, they would know." He inhales sharply, then taps his horse with his heels and breaks into a gallop. Over his shoulder, he calls, "Everything has changed, Alana. Everything."

For a moment, I simply sit, staring as Eldrion races away from me. But then I lean into my horse's neck, stroke her mane, tap my heels, and follow suit.

We leave the city through the large archway in the Shadowkind Quarter.

We pass the stadium where the Gloomweavers sold me and the other Leafborne at auction. I remember the first time I saw Eldrion. I remember thinking my only problem was that I needed to survive a cruel elf lord who wanted to keep us as his prisoners.

And that memory leads me back to Finn. The first time he appeared in my chambers, tending my injured feet with such tender care. Unafraid to touch me. Unafraid to see me.

Pain grips my chest. I know what he is now, and I know it was all a lie. But that doesn't stop my heart from remembering how it loved him.

The pretend version of himself that he crafted so carefully is tattooed on my heart, and I am not sure I will ever be able to erase his poisonous ink from my soul.

I know he is evil.

I know he used me and betrayed me.

But perhaps he loved me, too.

Perhaps both things can be true?

THE DUSTY TRACK THAT LEADS THROUGH THE FIELDS beyond the city, towards the forests, billows beneath the horses' hooves as we canter in the direction of the trees. Frequently, I look up at the sky, wondering whether the storm clouds will begin to chase us or whether Finn will suddenly appear in the sky. A devil with wings. Blotting out the sun, and swallowing all that is good with his anger.

For a moment, pity settles in my gut.

Finn is doing this because he is angry. He is not evil. Or, at least, he was not.

If the things he showed me were true, and I believe they are because I know Eldrion, and I know what he is capable of, then does he not have a right to be angry?

He is doing this because he wants to free his people.

A flicker of hope ignites in my chest. If that's true, perhaps there is a way to get through to him. Perhaps I can make him see this is not the way. That he doesn't have to hurt anyone else.

I glance at Eldrion as I overtake him.

If we can reach the camp before Finn, and I can talk to him, look him in the eyes, make him remember who he is, then maybe . . . just maybe . . . I can stop my vision from becoming a reality.

Maybe I can save us all.

The horse is picking up speed when, suddenly, she whinnies and stumbles. She slows down, quickly, almost throwing me over her neck because I wasn't prepared for the sudden change in motion.

"Whoaaaa." I try to soothe her, but then I realise why she has stopped. "Maura?"

Standing in front of us, arms wide, Maura stares at me with steely eyes.

My heart races so fast I feel it might rip a hole in my chest. "What's happened? Where are the others?"

She lowers her arms, resting her hands on her hips as Eldrion comes to a stop beside me. She doesn't even look at him. "I have no idea what happened. I left the camp to try and stop you from doing something stupid." She looks up at me, disgust swimming in her eyes. "But it seems I was too late. Your stupidity began months ago. When you decided to trust a Shadowkind jester more than you trusted your own kin."

"Alana, don't react," Briony whispers. "She's trying to get you to—"

"And why would I trust you?" Indignation flares quickly in my chest as I stare down at the elder fae, but it is laced with hurt. The hurt I've felt over and over and over again since I was a child. Because, no matter what I do, I am never enough. "You have done nothing but—"

"We do not have time for this." Eldrion extends a hand to Maura, moving his horse towards her. "Are you coming with us or are we leaving you here? I do not care which option you choose."

Her eyes flash. She hates him. A deep, fiery hatred. But she takes his hand, flicks her wings, and jumps up onto the back of his horse. She does not hold on to him, even though she looks frail enough to topple over if the horse moves too quickly. Instead, she uses her wings to help her balance.

Eldrion doesn't say another word. He simply grunts, and continues towards the forest.

SEVEN

Alana

_____

*A*s soon as we reach the edge of the treeline, tar-like dread thickens in my veins. My limbs feel heavy. My wings curl in on themselves.

The smell.

Charred flesh, and fear.

The air is so dense with it that I can barely breathe.

Eldrion climbs down from his horse and takes its reins in his hand. Maura follows suit, her bare feet landing softly on the mossy ground. She shudders visibly, and wraps her arms around her waist. "By the stars," she breathes. "What happened here?" She turns to me. "What did he do?"

I close my eyes and try to push away the visions that are clambering to return. Beating against the backs of my eyes, blinding me to anything else. I can't move. I know I need to walk, but I can't seem to find the energy in my body to leave my mare's warm, safe back.

Eldrion strides to me and holds out a hand. The way he looks at me, it's as if he loathes me and yet wants to protect me at the same time.

I take it reluctantly, and hold on tight as I lower myself to the ground.

Still gripping his hand, unable to let go, I shake my head. "I can't."

"We have to," he growls.

"It's already happened. We're too late." Panic is rising in my chest. "I can feel it. Can't you feel it?"

Eldrion looks down at me. He is so tall, and so broad, and so powerful. And yet in this moment, I know there is nothing he can do to protect me. If Finn returns now, right now, we are at his mercy. Eldrion is weakened.

Right now? I am probably stronger than he is, and yet his hand holding mine feels so good. So needed.

I hate that I need him.

I have never needed anyone, and I certainly won't begin now.

Roughly, I tug out of his grip, help Briony down, and then stride towards the treeline. Shoulders back, legs steady.

I caused this, so I must face it.

Yet, as soon as I set foot in the darkness between the trees, I waver. I have no idea how I'm going to force myself to confront what Finn has done.

Because he has, undoubtedly, done something terrible.

Unspeakable.

Unfixable.

My thoughts of getting here before it happened now seem foolish. Like so many other things I have done, and thought, and seen, and been in my life.

What made me think I could change his mind, even if I did arrive before he . . .?

I can't even form the thoughts.

I see them. I see what he did, but I can't allow myself to think them. It's too much.

I walk steadily forward, towards the campsite I left less than two days ago, and hold my head high. Watching me from the back, I want Eldrion to think I am brave, and strong. I want Maura to see that, too. Because she, above all others, has only ever seen me as a pariah.

And, despite knowing I shouldn't care, I still so desperately want to prove myself to her.

"Have you considered what we will do if he's still in the camp?" she says, stepping up beside me.

She is shorter than me, and fragile looking. All sharp angles and paper-like skin. Pale with dark blue veins on her hands and arms. She is hundreds of years old. She has seen more than I have and endured more than I have. She is strong. And yet, she is afraid, too.

"He's not there." I shake my head gravely. "He's gone. I'd know if he was still there."

Maura raises her eyebrows at me. "Did you truly love him?" she asks, with not a hint of kindness in her tone. "Or were you so blinded by lust that you tricked yourself into believing it was love?"

I press my lips together. I cannot answer her. I feel the way I did when I was a child, and when the other Leafborne demanded answers from me that I could not give them.

What are you, Alana? Are you reading my mind right now? What's wrong with you? Why are you so strange? What am I thinking right now? Did you do that? Did you make him do that? Did you make her cry? What is wrong with you?

I screw my eyes closed for a moment.

Eldrion is watching us. I can feel his steely gaze on me.

"The jester fooled us all," he says, striding forward. "This wasn't a plan he concocted overnight. Was it?" He looks at Briony.

She swallows hard and shakes her head. "No," she whispers. "Finn has been planning a rebellion over the Sunborne for hundreds of years. He manipulated us all. He made us think we were going to . . ." She hesitates, blinking quickly.

"Continue." Eldrion stops and folds his arms in front of his chest. "We are on the same side now, Briony, whether we like it or not. So, you have nothing to fear from me."

She studies his face. Somehow, even though he is offering her a truce, it comes out sounding like a threat.

"At first, it was just about escaping. Leaving the castle. That's why we built the tunnels. Then it became about you." A cold wind snaps through the trees, blowing Briony's dark hair across her face. She tucks it back and inhales deeply. "He wanted to remove you from power." She is choosing her words carefully. "But then . . ."

I step in because her words are thin and quivering, and she looks like she might begin to cry. "Then he changed the rules. He wanted to kill all Sunborne fae. Take over the city. Rule Luminael." A shudder runs through me. "That was when I decided to come to the castle to kill you. Because I thought it might stop him from taking it too far."

As I speak, Briony's eyes widen as if she can't believe I just admitted to Eldrion that I intended to assassinate him.

Maura purses her lips and tuts.

Eldrion nods slowly. "I see," he says. "A brave decision."

Maura tuts again. Does she see the flicker of heat between Eldrion and I? Does she think I have been manipulated yet again by a fae who makes my heart beat faster and my legs quiver?

With a small flick of his wings, Eldrion motions for us to continue walking. We sink into silence. The forest is becoming darker and colder.

I look down, and realise a thin grey mist is swirling around my feet.

It's becoming almost impossible to see.

My toes snag on something. I trip and reach out to steady myself, pulling pale purple light into my hands and casting it in front of me to illuminate the way.

I am about to keep walking when I realise what I tripped on.

A hand.

"Alana?" a choked whisper drifts up from beneath the fog.

"Raine?" I drop to my knees.

"Please help me."

I DROP TO MY KNEES BESIDE RAINE, MY HEART POUNDING. Her skin is ashen, her breath coming in ragged gasps. Cuts and burns mark her body, and her wings are tattered shreds.

"Eldrion!" I call out, my voice cracking.

To my surprise, he's by my side in an instant, and he looks concerned.

I didn't expect that; I expected him to shrug and look coldly past her. To tell me we need to move on quickly, and to leave her where she is. But his eyes drift to her pregnant belly, and I see his breath thicken in his throat.

"We should get her back to the castle," he says, his voice grim. He turns to Briony. "Can you take her?"

Briony nods, her face pale but tinged with relief that she does not have to progress any farther through the woods. "Of course."

"What if there are more survivors?" Maura asks curtly, looking at the horses.

Ignoring Maura, but speaking to Briony, Eldrion says, "When you return, tell the guards to send more horses to the woods. And send for my healer, also. She is a Sunborne. Elys. Send word and ask her to bring supplies and help to the castle."

As Eldrion gently lifts Raine into Briony's arms, I watch him and catch myself feeling a surge of warmth that takes me by complete surprise.

One show of tenderness doesn't undo all the hurt he has done, but it does show that there is something beneath his facade.

Something I didn't expect to see.

Briony takes the reins and looks back over her shoulder, nodding at me.

I catch Raine's hand. "Hold on, Raine. Please."

Before they leave, I close my eyes and reach out for her fears, and I soothe them with my mind. Raine visibly sighs. Her body relaxes. She turns towards me and her eyes flutter open.

She manages a weak, "Thank you," before Briony takes off, wings fluttering furiously behind her as the horse carries her and Raine back towards the castle.

I stand, my legs shaky. "We need to keep going," I say, dreading what we will find if we go farther.

Eldrion nods, and gestures for me to lead the way. Maura says nothing, but her eyes are hard as she follows us deeper into the forest.

As we approach the camp, the swirling fog beneath our feet thickens, and an eerie silence settles over us. No birdsong, no rustling of leaves – just an oppressive stillness that makes my skin crawl.

As we enter the clearing, though, the fog parts like a curtain.

My breath catches in my throat, and I hear Maura's sharp intake of air behind me.

A few days ago, the camp was teeming with life. There was noise, and chatter. Pen played his harmonica. The scent of our rations being cooked filled the air, and the playful crackle of the campfire danced in the background.

Now, there is no harmonica.

Bodies litter the ground, their forms twisted and broken, and bushes simmer, burning silently and filling the air with smoke.

I walk slowly forward, picking my way between them.

"They're all Leafborne." I am looking into faces I have known my entire life. The beautiful Leafborne fae, once so vibrant and full of life, now lie still and lifeless. All of them.

All of us.

Their wings, once shimmering, are charred and crumbling. Their bodies are covered in scratches and bruises. Faces are swollen and almost unrecognisable. Limbs are contorted into strange angles.

I stumble forward, my eyes darting from face to face, hoping against hope to find someone – anyone – still alive. But there's nothing. No movement, no sound, just the oppressive silence of death.

"No," I whisper, screwing my eyes closed as tears surge into the back of my throat. "No, no, no."

I search for Eldrion. He stands completely still, surveying the carnage. I cannot read the expression on his face.

"Finn did this," Maura's voice is cold and hard as she walks up from behind me. "Your precious jester. Your lover. This is what he's become. This is what you let into our midst."

I want to argue, to defend Finn, to defend myself, but the words die in my throat. Because she's right. Finn did this. The Finn I thought I knew, the Finn I loved, is gone. And this . . . this monster has taken his place.

How could I ever have thought I might stop him?

Grief surges through me so hard and fast I can barely breathe.

I shake my wings, and my arms, and try not to see the devastation, the death.

My heart hurts. It burns in my chest.

It turns to liquid, sloshing around beneath my ribs and making me feel as if my entire body is going to sink to the floor and never get up again.

But then my eyes catch on something. A scrap of white fabric, like the ribbons Finn used to twist and twirl in the air above the Sunborne court.

I walk to it slowly, and pick it up, turning it over in my hands.

As I stare at it, and memories drip through me like acid, the grief inside me hardens into something else. A cold fury that burns like ice.

Finn did this. And I will make him pay.

EIGHT

Eldrion

I have never seen Alana like this before. Yes, I saw her in my visions. But I have never been with her like this before.

I have known her only within the confines of the castle, and the one time we ventured outside of its walls it was not like this.

Here, surrounded by nature instead of concrete, she is radiant.

Even as we sit amongst the smouldering ruins of the Leaf-borne camp, her face smudged with smoke and tears, she glows.

Her auburn hair contrasts against the thick, velvety shades of green in the leaves and the grass and the foliage. Her skin seems smoother, paler, her freckles more vibrant.

Her eyes glisten as she turns to look at me.

She screws them closed and shakes her head. She presses a trembling palm to her chest. "I can feel it in the air," she whispers. "Their fear. It's . . ." She inhales sharply, her shoulders shaking.

I turn away. I can't look at her. A strange mixture of arousal and sympathy swells in my gut, and I don't know how to process it. So, I lock it down and focus on the scene in front of us.

When she starts to sob, loudly, however, I extend a wing and wrap it around her shoulders. For a moment, she remains stiff and brittle. Then she folds into me and rests her head on my shoulder.

As she lets the tears flow, and her entire body trembles against me, I try to modulate my thoughts and my breathing. All I want to do, all I can think about, is cradling her in my wings, taking her back to my bed, and coaxing her fears away by teasing her body until she sees stars.

Feeling those things as I stare at the charred remains of her kin feels both wrong and so incredibly right at the same time.

"I did this," she whispers. "I caused this. I trusted him. I had no idea. I never thought—" She lets out a small whimper that turns into a groan, and buries her head in her hands.

"Yes," Maura's voice drifts over from the shadows. When she emerges, her eyes are shining like sharp, deadly diamonds. On her frail, thin legs, she stalks over to us. Her wings flutter. She shakes her head, her silver hair long and loose over her shoulders.

Everything about her says elder. The Sunborne used to have them. My grandmother was one of them. But that was before we realised it was better to have one ruler instead of a group of well-meaning but often useless ones.

"You did cause this." She stands in front of Alana.

They are so incredibly different. The polar opposite of one another.

Alana is strength, and power, and curves, and youth, and beauty.

Maura is frail, and willowy. She looks as if she would be knocked over in the slightest of breeze, and there is nothing beautiful about her. She is hard, and sharp, and the lines of her face are not filled with kindness but with the bitterness that comes with knowing exactly what people are capable of in this world.

I hope I never see Alana's face become that knowing.

"You brought that fae into our midst. You trusted him. You bought his lies. You. The mighty empath who was supposed to save us all!" Maura scoffs, still towering above Alana.

Curling in on herself, Alana hangs her head and scrapes her fingers through her hair. I loosen my grip on her shoulder and stand, wings twitching with rage.

Maura holds up a dismissive palm and doesn't even bother to look in my direction. "This doesn't concern you," she says.

I step between her and Alana, physically nudging her back out of my way. "Oh, it does concern me, old woman. It definitely does."

"You think I'm afraid of you?" Maura spits. "You have

nothing left." She nods at me in disgust. "The jester took your powers. You are a shell."

The weight of her words hits my chest like a block of concrete and I almost physically recoil from her.

He did.

Finn took my power.

"Look at you." She nods at my wings. I curl one towards me and my breath turns to burning ice in my lungs. The tip. It is fading. "Soon, you'll be no more use than Kayan was when she took his powers from him." Maura sidesteps me, grabs Alana, and hauls her to her feet.

I am still staring at my wings. I fold them slowly forward. Both tips are the same. Paler. Thinner.

I am fading.

Hands on Alana's shoulders, Maura stares at her as she says, "I know what you are. I've always known. The great Lady of Luminael created you because she thought you were going to save us. She gave you the power to save us and what did you do? You frittered it away. The empath who couldn't tell she was being used by a demon."

When I look up, Alana is no longer crying. Her tears are drying on her cheeks. Her eyes have changed. Their corners twitch, and her forehead creases.

Her jaw stiffens.

"How dare you accuse me of frittering away my power. All my life, I was made to believe my power was a curse!"

"And so it was," Maura spits.

Alana swallows forcefully, then moves her hand and places it on top of Maura's. She squeezes. Then grips harder, her knuckles whitening with the pressure as she forcefully prises Maura's fingers away from her shoulder.

"Don't ever touch me again," Alana says. She draws herself up taller. Her wings crackle. Purple electricity flickers on their tips, and a deep purple smoke begins to gather around her feet. "He might have lost his powers, but I have not."

Maura stands firm, but her gaze shifts to the floor and she watches the purple smoke curling towards her.

Alana reaches out with both hands and physically pushes the old woman away from her. Maura stumbles and falls to the ground. Now, she really does look afraid.

That feeling is back. The pride, the arousal, the desire to fight for her and protect her.

I should intervene.

But I want to see where this ends.

Alana's eyes flash with something so familiar I feel it strike me in my gut. Rage. Power.

She looms over Maura, who stares up at her as if she always expected this moment and is resigned to what's about to happen. The purple smoke thickens, swirling around Alana's feet and creeping towards the elder fae. Maura's eyes widen but she says nothing. She just stares, almost daring Alana to take it too far.

I want to see Alana reclaim what this evil old witch took from her.

But I also know what will happen if Alana loses control.

I've been there, and I can't let it happen.

I won't let Alana's rage consume her, no matter how justified it may be.

This isn't her.

It might be me, but it is not her.

I put a firm hand on her shoulder. She flinches at my touch, her gaze never leaving Maura. "Alana," I command, "if you let anger control you, it's a slippery slope."

For a moment, she remains rigid, her magic crackling along her wings and intensifying. Then, slowly, she turns to face me. I expect to see pain and confusion, and perhaps it's there somewhere, but mostly what I see is anger. "She—"

"I know," I interrupt. "But this isn't the way, and it isn't safe here."

Alana's shoulders sag, and the purple smoke begins to dissipate. She nods, closing her eyes and taking a deep, shuddering breath. "You're right," she whispers, her voice barely audible over the crackling of the nearby flames. "I just . . ."

She walks past Maura towards the centre of the camp. Remnants of tents and the bodies of her kin scatter the ground.

I want to comfort her. In this moment, the desire to pull her into my arms, my wings wrapping around her in a protective embrace, is almost too much to bear.

But that is not what we are to each other.

She will not bury her face in my chest, her body shaking with silent sobs as I stroke her hair. That is not what we do.

She might forget occasionally, but she hates me and everything I have done. And I hate her for making me want to be something other than what I am.

"It's not your fault," is all I manage to say. "You couldn't have known."

I stand beside her, and feel my wings droop. They are tired. I am tired.

Behind us, Maura has risen to her feet and is now sitting on a tree trunk, leaning forward onto her knees, not speaking.

Alana seems lost in her own thoughts. I can almost see them flitting across her face. Until a faint sound catches her attention.

I hear it too.

It's coming from nearby, a moan that sounds like someone in pain.

Alana spins around, her brow furrowed in concern. "Did you hear that?"

I nod, and together we move towards the source of the noise. There, amidst the smouldering ruins, lies a Leaf-borne fae. Tree branches are covering their body, but they move beneath the debris and moan again.

Alana gasps, dropping to her knees beside them, and pulls aside the foliage. "Pen?" She sweeps a hand across his brow and leans down, holding her cheek over his mouth.

"He's breathing." She looks up at me. "We have to help him."

I turn to Maura, who is standing a few paces away now with her hands on her hips. She's watching us warily, her earlier animosity replaced by a grim determination.

"Take him back. Follow Briony. Alana and I will wait for more horses."

If Maura is grateful, she does not show it. She doesn't even nod in recognition of what I've said.

I whistle for my horse, who comes trotting over dutifully. Carefully, I lift Penn onto his back, securing him as best I can. Then I stand back as Maura positions herself behind him.

When they have gone, Alana and I search the rest of the camp. We examine every body, searching for anyone else who might have survived.

There is no one.

"Two," Alana breathes, steadying herself on the trunk of a nearby oak tree. "Only two survived."

I lace my fingers together behind my back and unfurl my wings. They ache in a strange way, as if they've been flat against my back for too long and need to be stretched.

I glance at them, notice their fading edges, and breathe in deeply. I can't allow myself to think about what it will mean if I don't take my powers back from Finn.

As if she can read my mind, Alana turns to me and says, "Do you think you can get them back? If we get close enough to him? Do you think I could take them and channel them back into you? Is there a spell?"

I shake my head. "Not that I know of. There might be something in the library where I found my mother's journal."

"Then we should go there."

"Maybe." I turn away from her and look out at the camp. Would she really help me reclaim my magic? Or would she want to see me disintegrate in front of her eyes? After everything that has happened, I wouldn't blame her if she did.

"Where are the others?" she asks. She's talking to me as if we are friends. The animosity in her tone temporarily displaced by the need for someone to trust.

"The Shadowkind were hiding with you?"

She nods. "They kept themselves separate from us, mostly. But yes, they were here."

"Finn spared his own kind," I mutter, my mind returning to the demons in my vision, more certain now than ever before that this is what Finn intends to do. I'm about to say more when I realise Alana is staring at her hands. They are covered in blood, and her face is stained with remnants of smoke.

Her hair, her skin, her entire body shows traces of what happened here. Of how she knelt over her kin and tried to revive them. And how she failed.

Suddenly realising she has the memory of her dead friends' lips on hers, from where she desperately tried to breathe life back into those with the least mutilated bodies, she wipes her mouth furiously with the back of her hand.

Panic ignites in her eyes. She tugs at the top of her tunic, her face flushing, her breath quickening.

"Alana . . ."

"I need it off me . . ." She looks down at her hands and her arms, shaking them as if she might free herself of the blood that is drying on her skin.

"The lake." I meet her eyes, and hold her gaze. But she is lost in panic now. She starts to pace up and down, taking deep, shuddering breaths that make her entire body quiver.

She is muttering something under her breath, but I can't hear what she's saying. At her feet, purple smoke starts to curl upwards and outwards.

I stride towards her, pushing my way through it and trying not to notice the shockwaves of pain that travel up through my body as the smoke makes contact with my legs.

I've seen Alana's powers. I've felt them. If she loses herself in panic, bad things could happen.

Grabbing her by her waist, I haul her over my shoulder. She starts to kick and scream and beat her fists against my chest.

I ignore the pummelling and stride away from the clearing towards the lake. The entire way, she shouts. The shouts turn to sobs, interspersed with words I can't interpret. I hear her say "Kayan" and my stomach clenches.

Then she descends into sobs again.

By the time we reach the water, she is still battling against my hold, and the purple smoke is up to my waist, squeezing me tightly. So, I wade in.

I keep going until the water is up to my chest, and then I drop her.

She falls beneath the surface and emerges spluttering.

Her eyes widen, and she inhales sharply as the cold makes contact with her.

"What are you doing?" she yells at me.

I say nothing, just watch as she fights to compose herself again.

Her tunic is plastered to her skin, her hair wet and hanging in thick tendrils on her shoulders. She moves her arms through the water, keeping herself afloat, and slowly – slowly – the panic fades.

"Why did you do that?" she asks, this time quieter, more like a whisper.

"You're covered in blood. You need a bath." I slip my hand beneath the water and take her arm. When I lift it up, water skims down it, dancing on the surface of her skin, making invisible rivers which flow over the blood that is already fading.

"Are you trying to be funny right now?" She quirks an eyebrow at me. Her strength is returning.

"I am not a funny man," I reply.

At that, she laughs. A burst of warmth that makes me, despite my better judgement, smile.

I'm still holding her arm.

I move closer to her. My wings are trailing in the water behind me.

With my eyes fixed on hers, I lift her arm to my mouth and kiss the spot below her wrist. I swirl my tongue over the blood, keeping her gaze while I clean it from her skin.

I will never understand how, in an instant, we can go from hating each other to wanting each other.

It happens so suddenly, every time, that I am neither prepared for it or able to stop it.

Alana watches me, not pulling away but not leaning into me either.

When I reach the inside of her elbow, and drag my tongue over the soft skin, she reaches out and pushes her fingers through my hair. Then, sighing, she tilts my face up towards her and kisses me.

Her lips are soft and searching. But then they become furious.

Her legs are around my waist. She's grabbing the back of my neck, her tongue is caressing mine.

I hold her still for a moment, then I reach up and rip open her tunic.

NINE

Alana

---

*E*ldrion tears open my tunic with a force that takes my breath away. It hangs open, exposing my breasts, falling off my shoulder.

He doesn't move, just stares at me and releases a low growl.

I lean back, deliberately allowing him a better view. He lifts a purposeful finger. It is wet, and when it makes contact with my nipple, a low whimper escapes my lips.

For a long moment, Eldrion simply stares at me and uses his fingers to tease me. He makes circles around my nipple, then wider, not touching it at all, then he squeezes gently. Then, drawing a gasp from my lips, he slaps me with a firm, open palm.

The shock of pain on my breast makes me groan.

I want more.

His eyes flash.

He dips his head to my other breast and draws my nipple into his mouth. He bites a little, causing the same shudder of pain to shake my entire body. I dig my nails into his shoulders. My legs are around his waist and I can feel him stiffening beneath me. I grind my pelvis down onto him and he pulls me closer, growling as if he cannot physically have me close enough.

Below the surface, my pants are soaked and clinging to my skin. There is no way I'll be able to pull them down over my hips, and the thought that I can't enter him right now makes me cry out with frustration.

Eldrion's eyes flash again. He knows what I want.

He dips his arms below the surface and finds the catch on my waist. He unfastens it. His shoulders ripple. He holds my gaze as he pulls, forcing the water to bend to his bidding through pure brute strength.

It occurs to me that I could help him. I have water magic; Kayan's magic. But watching him do it this way, and feeling his strength without his power is sending waves of arousal through my entire body.

When my pants are gone, he pushes his own down over his hips, grabs me, and enters me without hesitation.

My legs tighten around him, gripping him with my thighs.

His warmth merges with the coolness of the water, deep inside me, making me grab onto him and tip my head back.

As his lips trail down my throat, I whimper and pull him closer. I need him deeper, fuller, faster.

And he knows it.

He fucks me the way I need to be fucked.

Hands, and teeth, and lips, and skin, and water slapping between us.

He teases my breasts, alternating between softness and hardness. Each time he draws gasps of pain from my lips, he smirks. And it makes me want to throttle him and fuck him harder at the same time.

His hand moves to my throat. His fingers tease me, threatening to close around my neck, but then dropping down to the small of my back to hold me against him.

When he next returns his mouth to my breasts, I know I'm going to come.

I whisper to him and, in that moment, a flicker of tenderness flashes through in his touch. He meets my eyes and nods at me. "You can do it, Alana. Let it all go."

I hold the sides of his face, staring into his eyes as the pleasure builds.

He bites his lower lip. He wants to come, too. He needs to come, but he's waiting. He wants me to tip over the edge.

When my body finally does implode on itself, fireworks shaking my thighs and skittering down my spine, Eldrion lets go, too. I feel him swell and release inside me, and it intensifies my pleasure even without me having to reach out and search for it.

I am panting, clinging on to him, soaking wet and starting to shiver, when I see a blue shimmering light on the shore. It moves quickly, but I know what it is.

Kayan. He was watching.

And he saw me fucking the man who killed him.

ELDRION ATTEMPTS TO CARRY ME TO THE SHORE, BUT I push him away. I unfurl my legs from around his waist and stride awkwardly through the water towards solid ground.

When I reach the beach, I'm already pulling my completely sodden pants up to my waist. I hold on to them tightly, and exhale slowly, sending the water particles merging and trickling back into the lake, leaving my clothes dry.

As Eldrion steps up beside me, he raises an eyebrow as if he thinks I might do the same for him.

I will not.

I am searching for Kayan, scanning the trees for the blue light that told me he'd seen the most despicable betrayal.

I thought he had gone, that I would never see him again. So, to know he came back for me and was greeted by the sight of me and Eldrion – the man who ended his life – is almost too much to bear.

Perhaps Maura was right about me.

Perhaps it really would be better for everyone if I wasn't here anymore.

I try to breathe out slowly, focus on anything but the tingle that still rests between my thighs, and the way Eldrion felt inside me, and the sounds he made as he fucked me.

He flutters his wings.

They are different. Faded. But he is somehow still so powerful. I don't understand it, and I don't understand why my body responds to him the way it does.

I wish it didn't.

With my entire being, I wish I could stop feeling this way.

But when I look at him now, dripping wet, his shirt open, his pants low on his hips exposing his flat, sculpted stomach and the line of hair that leads down to his . . .

I shake my head and turn away.

Get a grip, Alana.

Get a grip.

As if he knows exactly what I'm thinking, Eldrion's lip curls into a smile. He puts his hand on my shoulder. It is not kind, but it is not too firm either.

"We can talk about what just happened if you want to, but it doesn't have to mean anything." He raises an eyebrow at me. "Just like all the other times don't have to mean anything either."

"You gave me a release I needed." I tip my chin up and stare at him. "That's all."

"Indeed." He adjusts his shirt as if there's anything he can do to make himself look less dishevelled when he's still soaking wet. But then he tilts his head and looks towards the trees. "Do you hear that? I think our backup has arrived."

I follow him to the edge of the treeline. We have almost reached it when four large black horses arrive. On one of them sits a Shadowkind guard I do not recognise. He looks pale and clammy, and when he nods back towards the forest and opens his mouth to speak, no sound comes out.

"I will explain, but not now," Eldrion barks, jumping up onto the largest horse. "There are no more survivors. We return to Luminael."

The guard purses his lips. He looks as though he's trying not to vomit. His nose wrinkles with the memory of charred flesh, and the gesture brings back my own memory.

To shift it, I jump quickly onto my own horse, tap its sides, and gallop away.

I race as fast as I can.

Through the forest, not looking at the bodies or the debris, barely breathing until I have escaped the fog and the death.

Then across the meadows towards Luminael. Through the streets towards the castle.

I could leave. Right now, I could take a new direction and race away from here and never have to see Eldrion or this place or Finn ever again.

Except, I can't. Because I caused this, so I have to try to undo it.

And because I know, deep down, that even if I did run . . . Finn would find me.

He would not let me go that easily.

When I reach the castle, there is more movement than I have seen in a long time. Briony greets me, reaches up and helps me down from the horse.

"How are they?" I ask, hurrying along beside her. "Where are they?"

"The healer came, and she's helping them."

"Raine's baby?"

Briony blinks at me, presses her lips together, and swallows forcefully. "The healer is trying to save them both."

I stop, gripping Briony's hand tightly. "I'm so sorry."

"So am I," she says. "We both believed Finn was something different."

I pull her towards me and breathe her in. I have never had a true friend before. Not until now. She is the one constant in everything that is happening. "Thank you," I whisper.

Briony pulls back, still holding on to my upper arms. "Promise me we'll stick together," she says. "Promise we have each other, Alana, because if we don't . . ."

"You don't want to go with him and the others?" The question leaves my mouth before I've really thought it through, and causes Briony to frown at me and shake her head.

"Of course I don't want to go with him," she says. "I don't want to see him again. Ever. And I certainly don't want any part of what he's planning."

"I'm sorry." I inhale slowly and hold the breath in my lungs. "I know. I'm sorry."

Briony squeezes my hand. "You should go clean up. Take a minute. Then come and see Raine."

I am about to head back inside when I realise I don't really know where I should be going. Are my chambers still my own?

I am still trying to decide when Eldrion clatters into the courtyard, his horse's hooves heavy and urgent. He swings down while she is still in motion, and spins around quickly.

Behind him, a group of Sunborne fae enter the courtyard.

"My lord." A woman at the front of the group dips into a curtsey, then looks up at the sky. She is polite, but the expression on her face says she will not be dismissed without answers. "What exactly is happening here?"

TEN

Eldrion

—————

*S*uranna, the Sunborne who has been trying to flirt me into marriage for the past two hundred years, approaches with a quiet confidence. There was a time when I found her attractive, but that was before I realised there was absolutely nothing behind her eyes.

No humour, no fight, no spirit.

She is all poise and grace, and it is terribly fucking boring.

But now, as her eyes turn to the sky above the castle, her facade cracks a little. Not to show anything worthy of intrigue, but to show a flicker of some emotion at least.

Even if it is fear.

"What happened here, Eldrion?" she asks, her voice cool and smooth. Honey on snow. "We all saw the clouds gather. We felt something shift. There are rumours that a . . ." She hesitates, glances at the Shadowkind guards and servants who are moving through the courtyard, and lowers her voice. "There are rumours that a demon was seen in the sky. Everyone is in hiding, my lord. Only a few of us dared even leave our houses to come and speak to you."

I roll my tongue over my teeth.

Alana had been about to walk away from me, but she is still here. Watching. Her arm hooked in Briony's as if they are sisters or, at the very least, friends who have known each other so long they have become family.

"There was an incident, but it is under control, Suranna."

Suranna tucks a strand of jet-black hair behind her ear. Her dark skin glows in the sunlight, and the way she chews her lower lip reminds me why I found her so attractive when we first met.

"I am not going to be dismissed with meaningless answers," she says firmly. Behind her, a few others speak up.

If there is one thing Sunborne do well, it is composure. We hold ourselves above all others, and it is something we carry on our shoulder as we move through the world – the calming knowledge that we are the most powerful creatures in the kingdom.

What will happen if they learn this is no longer the case? Because, undoubtedly, at this moment Finn is stronger than them.

He took my power and he amplified it.

And if they realise I am powerless, except for a useless ability to see flashes of a future that may or may not come to pass, will they still want me as their leader? Or will they elect another?

A sensation I can't name settles beneath my skin.

I will not lose my throne to these people. Not after everything I've sacrificed trying to keep the kingdom safe.

I draw back my shoulders, keeping my wings pinned at my back because if she sees them, she really will know that I am lying.

"It was a Leafborne." Alana steps forward, hands on hips.

Briony frowns at her.

Suranna turns her head slowly to look at Alana, but her expression remains unreadable.

"A Leafborne escaped and returned with dark magic. They tried to attack the castle. Eldrion fought them off."

Slowly, Suranna looks back at me. "Who is this fae? Who calls you by your name, and not by your title, and answers for you, Lord Eldrion?"

"She is an empath," I answer quickly. "She has been advising me, and her word is to be trusted."

For a moment, Suranna looks as if she might challenge me. The crowd behind her quiets, waiting for her to speak. "An empath?" She frowns. "I recognise you from court. You have attended some of Lord Eldrion's feasts?"

Alana tilts her chin up, suddenly a picture of grace and regality. "Indeed."

"I have never encountered an empath before." Suranna's eyes twitch as though she is wondering whether she should attempt to hide her thoughts from the woman in from of her.

Then a slow, strange smile parts her lips. She steps towards Alana and nods at her. It is a display of respect, and yet no respect lives in her gaze. None.

"Thank you for clearing that up," she says calmly before turning back to face me. "Am I to assume there will be a feast at the castle again soon? We have missed our jester."

I sense Briony stiffen and pray she has not given us away with an uncontrolled display of emotion.

"Of course." I nod firmly, and reach out for Suranna's hand. I kiss her knuckles and look up at her, smiling. "And I would be honoured if, at the next banquet, you would sit with me at the high table, Suranna. It has been too long since we spent some quality time in each other's company."

A smile flutters on Suranna's lips. She does not allow it to turn into the kind of smile that brightens her face, but she does dip her head a little and flutter her eyelashes.

I glance at Alana.

At least my charm is still effective with some.

"That would be wonderful," she replies smoothly.

I do like her voice, but it is not like Alana's. It does not have the spirit or the tenacity that hers does.

"Then, please, do not let me keep you from your day." I extend an arm, gesturing towards the archway at the rear of the courtyard. "And expect to hear word very soon about the next gathering."

Suranna looks at me over her shoulder as she leaves. Her eyes move to Alana, then quickly back to me. If she suspects I am lying, she does not show it on her face.

"Soon," she calls, raising her arm. But as she is almost through the archway, she stops and looks up at the sky again. "And shall we expect the storm clouds to disperse soon, too?"

"Of course." I raise a hand and wave. "I will see to it immediately."

When they are gone, and far enough away that I will not be heard, I spin around and storm towards Alana. "I was handling it," I bark at her.

"No," she says calmly. "You were not. And I'm guessing that a city full of panicked Sunborne is the last thing we need right now. At least until we have figured out what to do next."

I open my mouth to speak, but she cuts me off with a vicious shake of her head. "I need to go and see my friends." She turns back to Briony and, once again, hooks her arm through the smaller fae's. "Can we go and see them now?"

Briony nods and pats Alana's hand. "Of course. Follow me."

I want to follow her. Everything inside me wants to follow her, always.

But I don't. I just stand and watch her cross the courtyard as if she always belonged here, and was always meant to roam free within my walls.

When I arrive back to my chambers, all I can see is her.

She is everywhere here, and the thought of her returning to her own room tonight makes me feel something I can't explain.

My mother's journal still lies on the floor in the middle of the room. I pick it up and flip through the pages. Her words feel different now. Meaningless, and yet more meaningful than anything else I can hold onto.

I set it down on the desk and press my palm to the cover.

And then I feel it.

A vision.

Racing towards me.

I'm floating, suspended in darkness. Flashes of light pierce the blackness. Images flood my mind.

Finn. Wings spread wide, blocking out the sun. His eyes glow red. A wicked smile twists his face. Shadows swirl around him, my shadows, writhing like living smoke.

They belong to him now. He owns them, and they taunt me with their absence.

The Shadowkind gather below. Hundreds, maybe thousands. Their faces a mix of fear and awe. Finn raises his arms. The shadows respond, converging into a swirling vortex.

It spins faster, growing larger. A yawning chasm of darkness. Finn's voice booms, echoing, weaving into the corners of my mind. "Step into your destiny!"

A Shadowkind approaches. Hesitant at first, then with purpose. He reaches the edge of the vortex. Pauses. Looks back at Finn. Finn nods. The Shadowkind jumps.

The shadows engulf him. His scream cuts off abruptly.

Moments pass. The vortex churns.

My heart races. I want to look away and leave this place and never return, but it's as if I am standing outside myself watching and I cannot make myself move.

All I can do is watch, transfixed by the shadows.

As I stare at them, my heart matching the rhythm of the cyclone inside them, something emerges. Not the Shadowkind who entered. Something . . . else.

Taller. Broader. Wings like solid blocks of night. Eyes glowing crimson.

No longer fae. A demon.

A demon like Finn.

The creature roars. Others step back, but their eyes shine with hunger. They know now what they can become, and they are desperate to step into their fate.

Another Shadowkind approaches. Then another. And another.

They leap into the vortex. Screams cut short.

Demons emerge. An army growing by the minute.

Finn laughs. The sound chills me to my core. The scene shifts. A city. Luminael. My city.

Sunborne fae fill the streets.

The sky darkens. Wings blot out the sun. Finn's demon army descends.

Chaos. Screaming. Blood on cobblestones. Sunborne fall by the dozens, their light extinguished.

Suranna stares up at me with dead, unblinking eyes. There is a tear on her cheek. Her light is gone.

Finn strides through the carnage. Untouched. Triumphant. He reaches the castle. Kicks down the doors.

Inside, a throne room. Two thrones. One for Alana and one for me. We sit and stare at him as he strides towards us. From the ceiling, remnants of his jester's ribbons sway and flutter. He grabs hold of them, twists his arms effortlessly into them, and almost dances on the air as he swings towards us.

Alana watches him with wonder in her eyes. She breathes his name, and I hate the way it sounds on her lips.

Finn drops the ribbons. His shadows crawl towards him from the corners of the room, they reach me first, but Alana is still smiling at Finn.

They are taking me. They are suffocating me. I call to her for help, but she just stares at him. And stares at him.

He kisses her. He asks her if she will stand beside him and she whispers yes as she opens her dress for him.

While I suffocate on the throne beside her, Alana lets Finn take her body. She calls his name again and again. And when they are done, he kicks me to the floor. The shadows swallow me up.

He takes the throne. His demons bow before him. The

vision blurs, speeds up. Cities falling. Kingdoms crumbling. Darkness spreads across the land like a plague.

THE VISION FADES, LEAVING ME GASPING FOR BREATH, MY body drenched in cold sweat. Finn's demonic form, wreathed in shadows and destruction, lingers in my mind. The scale of his plans, the sheer devastation he intends to unleash, is beyond anything I could have imagined.

And while I am normally left in doubt, trying to piece together my visions and interpret what they mean, this time it could not be any clearer.

Finn intends to turn the Shadowkind into demons, form an army, and take over the city. And if he does, the carnage will be unimaginable.

As I try to sift through the snippets of information that now swim behind my eyes, I cannot shift the image of Alana giving herself to him like that.

Would she really want to be by his side?

She owes me nothing, but would she betray herself like that?

I stagger to the window, bracing myself against the sill as I gulp in the cool night air. The citadel sleeps below. The Sunborne cannot be oblivious to the storm that is coming. Come the morning, they will be here, demanding answers for what happened in the sky above the castle.

And I will have to find a way to explain it to them.

"Eldrion."

The voice sends a chill down my spine. I turn slowly, already knowing what I'll see.

Who I'll see.

My mother stands in the centre of the room, shimmering and translucent in the moonlight. Her eyes, which I remember as being so cold and distant, now brim with an emotion I've never seen in them before. Regret.

"Mother," I say, my voice hoarse. "Have you come to apologise?" I shake the journal at her.

She lowers her head, taking a step towards me. "No, my son. I've come to confess."

I laugh bitterly. "Confess? Now? When it's far too late? I know everything. I read it in here! All the things you never told me. The pieces that would have made everything make sense."

"I didn't know," she whispers. "I swear to you, I didn't know it would come to this."

"Then what did you think would happen?" I snarl, my anger rising. "When you twisted an innocent child in her mother's womb, and when you created a weapon without thought for the consequences?"

My mother's form flickers, as if buffeted by the force of my rage. "I saw the darkness coming," she says. "I saw our kingdom in ruins, our people destroyed. I thought . . . I thought I could prevent it."

"By creating Alana? By burdening her with power she never asked for, never understood? And by telling no one?"

"I believed she would be our salvation," my mother pleads. "A force of light to push back the shadows."

I stride towards her, my wings flaring. "And instead, you've given those shadows form. You've handed Finn the key to unlock his true nature, to become the very demon you feared!"

She flinches, and for a moment, I see the proud, infallible woman I grew up with crumble. "I was wrong," she whispers. "So terribly wrong. I let my fear cloud my judgement, and now . . ."

I should feel sorry for her. But I don't. I look at her and all I see is the woman who made my life a misery, and who made me grow up feeling less.

"Now we all pay the price," I finish for her. The anger that's been building inside me finally explodes. "You should have left well enough alone! You should have trusted in us, in me, to face whatever came! Instead, you played with forces beyond your understanding, and look what you've done."

"I've spent my entire life trying to protect this kingdom, trying to live up to the legacy you left behind. And all along, you'd already sown the seeds of our destruction." I toss the journal at her and it slices right through her shimmering form. "You could have told me. If you'd told me."

"Eldrion, please," she begs, reaching out a ghostly hand. "We can still fix this. Together, we can—"

"No!" I roar. "You've done enough. More than enough. You no longer have any place here, Mother. Not in this castle, not in this world, and certainly not in my life. You are not welcome. You never have been—"

The room falls silent. I stand there, chest heaving. She is gone.

If she was ever here to begin with.

Alone once more, I turn back to the window. The sun is setting now, and it would be beautiful, if I didn't know the darkness that's coming.

ELEVEN

Finn

---

*T*he salty sea breeze whips through my hair as I lead our group along the shoreline. Yarrow walks beside me, his eyes constantly scanning the horizon for any sign of danger. Behind us, a long line of Shadowkind fae trudge through the sand. They do not know whether they want to be here or not, but soon they will understand what it is I am offering them.

"You sure about this, Finn?" Yarrow mutters, his voice barely audible over the crashing waves.

I nod, keeping my eyes fixed on the cliffs ahead. "I have never been so sure of anything in my life." I turn to him and grin. "And you, my friend, will be the first to experience the power and the joy that is to come."

As we approach the towering cliffs, I spot the white, broken-away section of the cliff.

I don't know why I felt that this was the fitting place for our transformation. It is not a Shadowkind haunt; it belonged to the elves for centuries until they abandoned their care of it and decided to become keepers of secrets and lies in a very different way.

Perhaps it is because this is where I found the answers I had been looking for. Perhaps it is because it holds an ancient energy in its walls. Perhaps I just like old books.

"There." I point out the cave entrance to Yarrow. He nods, then turns to relay instructions to the others.

I pause at the mouth of the cave, allowing my eyes to adjust to the darkness within. The air feels heavy, charged with that familiar elvish energy. "Everyone stay close," I call out.

We move deeper into the cave, the sound of our footsteps echoing off the damp walls. The farther we go, the more the darkness seems to press in around us. I can hear the nervous whispers of the Shadowkind behind me, their fear palpable in the enclosed space.

Finally, we reach the underground pool. Its surface is like black glass, reflecting nothing but more darkness.

"What now?" Yarrow asks, eyeing the water suspiciously.

I take a deep breath and turn to him, my red eyes glowing in the darkness. "We swim." I gesture to the pool. "You first, my friend."

For the first time since I returned to the camp, Yarrow hesitates. But then he steels himself, sets his jaw in a determined line, and dives in without a second thought.

"Who is next?" I turn to the others.

No one speaks. No one wants to be the next to volunteer.

"You think I would bring you all the way here to end your lives in a dark, dank cave? I would have killed you in the forest if that was my intention." I jerk the arm of the fae closest to me and, without hesitating, throw her into the pool.

Then I unleash the shadows. They form a solid wall behind the group and start to gently nudge them forward.

They move with slow, petrified feet. And as each one reaches me, I am forced to hurl them in.

When the last one is gone, disappearing with a gasp and a splash, I inhale deeply. The scent of the damp cave fills my nostrils. Sea air, and freedom.

Then, I dive into the pool after them.

The cold hits me like a physical blow, driving the air from my lungs. I kick downwards, pushing through the inky blackness. Just when I think my lungs might burst, I feel it – a strange current, pulling me forward.

I'm engulfed in a blinding purple light. I squeeze my eyes shut, disoriented. When I open them again, I find myself standing in the same circular room that gave me what I never thought was possible.

The truth.

With towering bookshelves that stretch up into shadows, it is a place of calm and quiet.

The others seem more relaxed standing here, as if they are surprised I brought them somewhere so beautiful.

"By the stars," Yarrow breathes. "It's real. The Elven Archives?"

I nod. "It's real, my friend. And this is where I found the truth about our kind."

I stride over to the small table near the centre of the room. On its surface lies a single book, bound in deep blue leather.

I lay my hands on its cover and breathe in the memory of the words that lie within. "Do you know what this text is?" I ask, looking up at the watching crowd. Just twenty of them.

Twenty Shadowkind to begin to revolution.

What a delicious thought.

No one answers me.

"This text is called *The Rise and Fall of the Shadowkind*," I read aloud. "*A Treatise on the Darkest Chapter of Our History*."

Yarrow appears at my shoulder, peering down at the text. "What does it say?"

A hush falls over the library and now, in this moment, it is as if the others have forgotten that I have changed.

They don't see my new face or my glowing eyes.

They trust me.

They gather around, hanging on my every word as I begin to read to them.

"In the ancient annals of our kingdom, there exists a race of fae known as the Shadowkind. Born with wings as dark as night and hearts to match, these creatures were once the scourge of our realm, their very existence a blight upon the land.

"It is said that in the early days, the Shadowkind lived amongst the other fae, their true nature hidden beneath a veneer of civility. But as they reached the age of fifty, a strange and terrible transformation would occur. Their wings, once small and unremarkable, would grow and mature, becoming vast and powerful. And with this physical change came a darkness of the soul, a corruption that twisted their very being.

"The Shadowkind were beings of pure evil, their magic fuelled by the shadows that clung to their wings. They rampaged across the kingdom, spreading terror and destruction wherever they went. The other fae, the Leafborne, the Mountainside, and Waterweavers, lived in constant fear, never knowing when the next attack would come.

"In those dark days, the Sunborne lived apart, sequestered in their citadel like monks in a monastery. They were the guardians of light and, along with the elves, the keepers of ancient knowledge. But they did not interfere in the affairs of the outside world. And so, for generations, the kingdom suffered under the reign of shadows.

"Until a hero arose from among the Sunborne. The first of the line that would become known as the Lords and Ladies of Luminael. This brave and noble fae, whose name has been lost to history, looked upon the suffering of the kingdom and knew that something had to be done.

"With a small but devoted band of followers, he ventured forth from the citadel and took the fight to the Shadowkind. The war that followed was long and brutal, the forces of light and darkness clashing in a conflict that threatened to tear the very fabric of the world asunder.

"But in the end, the Sunborne prevailed. The Shadowkind were defeated, their armies scattered, their power broken. But the hero knew this was not enough. As long as the Shadowkind's wings remained unbound, as long as their dark magic was allowed to flourish, the kingdom would never truly be safe.

"And so, a practice began. The Shadowkind, now subjugated and enslaved, had their wings bound as soon as they fledged. Tight, constricting ropes that prevented their wings from ever reaching maturity, and therefore from ever unleashing the evil that lurked within.

"This practice has continued for thousands of years, handed down from generation to generation of Sunborne rulers. It is a necessary cruelty, a harsh but vital measure to ensure the safety and prosperity of the kingdom. For without the bindings, the Shadowkind would rise again. Their dark magic would return, and the realm would once more be plunged into an age of terror and despair.

"This is the truth of our history, the dark secret that underlies the very foundation of our society. It is a heavy burden, a grim responsibility. But it is one the Sunborne, the descendants of that first great hero, must bear.

"For the sake of the kingdom, for the sake of all fae, the Shadowkind must remain bound. Their wings must never be allowed to spread. And those with shadow magic must beware; for if the magic of shadows is used on a bound fae, their power will be unleashed. Their demon form will rise. This is the curse of the bindings."

I close the book and wait while silence quivers in the air.

When I look up, several of the Shadowkind are crying.

A few others are shaking their heads, steely determination forming in their gazes.

In a gentle, soothing tone, I begin to speak once more. "For too long, we've lived in chains. But now we know the truth."

I hold the book up, my voice rising with passion. "This is our true history. And with it, we'll rewrite our future. We'll reclaim our power, our heritage. We'll show the Sunborne – show all of Luminael – what we truly are. I have already stolen Eldrion's power from him."

From the darkness between the bookcases, shadows creep free.

"And now I will give you some of that same power. I will unleash what is inside you all, so we can be truly free. Forever."

The library erupts in cheers, the sound echoing off the ancient walls. As I look out at the sea of faces, I see hope blazing in their eyes. Hope, and something darker. Something powerful.

From the front of the crowd, Yarrow raises his voice. "Hail Finn!" he cries, turning and gesturing for the others to join in. His voice booms into the air, so loud it causes a flutter of dust to drift into the air. "Hail the Shadow King!"

For a moment, the other Shadowkind seem stunned. But then, slowly, they take up the chant. "Hail Finn! Hail the Shadow King!"

Triumph surges inside me. This is what I was born for, what I was always meant to be. A leader. The one who will reshape the world in his own dark image.

"Yes," I say, my voice rising above the chanting. "Together, we will build a new kingdom. An empire of shadow and darkness, where the strong rule and the weak perish."

The Shadowkind roar their approval, their eyes gleaming with a newfound sense of purpose and destiny.

The Age of Shadow has begun, and I will be its king.

"So," I roar. "Who will be the first to embrace their destiny?"

TWELVE

Finn

———————

*S*hadows dance on the walls, cast by the flickering torches we've lit. The air is thick with tension and the acrid smell of fear mixed with excitement.

Yarrow stands beside me, his eyes gleaming with a mixture of apprehension and eagerness. He was always going to be the first. He has stood by me when all others doubted me.

I would never expect him to wait.

"Yarrow." I turn to him and place a firm hand on his arm. He has always been larger than me, and fiercer than me. But now I tower above him.

His eyes glisten with emotion.

"Are you ready to be the first? To show our people what we truly are?"

He nods, squaring his shoulders. "I am ready."

"It will hurt, brother."

"I am ready," he repeats through gritted teeth.

I gesture for him to step forward. Yarrow moves to the centre of the cavern, standing tall despite the bindings on his wings. The crowd falls silent, all eyes fixed on us.

"For this to work," I explain, "we need shadow magic. Magic that was stolen from us, just like our freedom." I look down at my hands, concentrating. The shadows around us seem to deepen, to coalesce. "Thanks to Eldrion, I have that magic."

I reach out, feeling the darkness respond to my call. It swirls around my fingers, cold and alive. With a deep breath, I direct it at Yarrow. The way it was directed at me when I jumped in front of Alana.

I aim to kill.

Except I know that will not happen.

Instantly, Yarrow is engulfed by shadows. They coil around his body like a cocoon. He drops to the ground, just as I did, and stares unblinking at the ceiling of the cavern.

Everyone falls silent.

"He's dead," someone mutters. "What did you do?"

For a moment, nothing happens. Then Yarrow lets out a scream that fills my core with frantic, joyful energy.

Here it comes.

The transformation.

His body contorts, his back arching at an impossible angle. I hear the sickening crack of bones breaking and reform-ing. His wings strain, then snap with a sound like thunder and grow larger, splaying out sideways as he cries out.

Gasps and cries of alarm rise from the onlookers. Some take a step back, but most are transfixed.

Yarrow's wings grow larger by the second. The dull grey turns to pitch black. His body grows too, muscles swelling and reshaping beneath his skin.

When he opens his eyes, they're glowing red.

Like mine.

The shadows recede, leaving Yarrow standing there, panting heavily. He looks down at his hands, flexing his fingers. Then he spreads his wings – his true wings – for the first time.

A gust of wind sweeps through the cavern, extinguishing half the torches. In the semi-darkness, Yarrow looks like something out of a nightmare. Or a dream.

"How do you feel?" I ask, my voice barely above a whisper.

Yarrow turns to me, a grin spreading across his face. It's not the smile I know – there's something feral about it, something dangerous. "Powerful," he growls, his voice deeper than before. "I feel . . . complete."

He raises his hand, and shadows dance across his palm. "I can feel the magic, Finn. It's . . . it's incredible."

I clap his shoulder and pull him into a firm, brotherly embrace.

It worked. There is nothing that can stop us now.

Turning back to the crowd, I spread my arms wide. "You see? This is what we were meant to be. This is our true form, hidden from us for generations. Who will be next?"

There's a moment of hesitation. Then, slowly, a young Shadowkind steps forward.

"I am," she says.

One by one, others step forward. The air fills with voices claiming their right to transformation.

I begin the process again, channelling the shadow magic into each volunteer. The cavern fills with screams of pain that gradually turn to cries of exultation. Wings unfurl, bodies reshape, eyes glow red in the darkness.

With each transformation, I feel the shadow magic within me grow stronger. It's intoxicating, this power. Part of me wonders if this is what Eldrion felt like all the time.

Does he miss it now it is gone?

Will he mourn it for the rest of his sorry days?

I hope so, even though those days are numbered.

As the last of the volunteers completes their change, I survey the cavern. Where once stood a group of subdued, bound Shadowkind, now a host of powerful beings fill the space. Their wings scrape the ceiling, their eyes gleam.

Yarrow approaches me, his footsteps unnaturally quiet despite his increased size. "What now, my king?" he asks, his voice a low rumble.

I meet his gaze.

"Now," I say, raising my voice and allowing it to rise and rise and echo and echo. "We take back what's ours. Luminael will tremble before us. The Sunborne will pay for what they've done." I pause, letting my words sink in. "And

Alana Leafborne . . . Alana will see what true power looks like."

THIRTEEN

Kayan

---

*S*eeing Alana like that, with Eldrion, made me feel numb. If I'd thought about it beforehand, I'd have assumed it would fill me with rage, or bile, or hatred.

But I feel none of those things.

Just emptiness.

I don't even think of the night we spent together. I don't see visions of Alana and I, bodies entwined, promising to love each other forever. I don't even see Eldrion's face as he threw me to my death.

I see nothing.

And I don't know if that's because I'm not really here or because it is too much to absorb.

When she sees me, that changes. Something shifts in my gut and uneasiness fills my lungs. She hates herself for wanting him and that is what hurts me.

To know she is giving herself to him and that afterwards she will be filled with disgust for herself; that is not something she should ever feel.

I follow them back to the castle. She is bristling with anger, and yet when she looks at him, there is something else simmering in her gaze. It is not affection. Is it need? The need to be close to him?

Perhaps in some strange way, he makes her feel safe amongst all this death and carnage and decay.

Approaching the citadel, I look up at the sky. It is still bruised with storm clouds. They hover ominously above the castle while the rest of the city rests beneath pale blue sky and fluffy white clouds.

They are an omen of what's to come. Because, undeniably, something is coming.

Finn has unleashed a darkness I haven't felt before.

And I realise now that this is my purpose. Whatever is coming, I was sent back to help.

Following them over the bridge and into the courtyard, remaining completely invisible even to Alana, I try not to let the thud of guilt settle beneath my ribs. Could I have stopped her trusting him? Would it have made a difference?

Something tells me it would not have; that all paths would have led to this even if I had made Alana see that Finn was not to be trusted.

When I see her embracing Briony, my heart lightens a little. At least she has one, true friend who can ground her. She needs that.

She has always been a deep thinker. She takes other people's emotions and her own and she dwells on them. She allows them to fester and turn her into something more muted than she should be.

Her parents and the elders of our village always tried to encourage her to ignore her power, bite down on it, keep it hidden and quiet and buried deep inside her.

I always felt as though they should do the opposite, and teach her how to use it.

Because fighting it has not helped anyone.

Used properly, her powers could help not just Alana but everyone else, too. The way she helped the Leafborne in the dungeon after my death.

She could be a healer. She could be something great.

If only they gave her the chance.

Perhaps after all this is over, I can help her see where her strength lies.

She is walking away from Eldrion with Briony when a group of Sunborne arrive at the gates. They have seen the clouds above the castle, and they want to know what is happening.

Eldrion tries to give them a half-answer, hoping to encourage them to leave without a fight for more truth. The woman he's speaking to does not believe him. She wants more, and I am shocked when it is Alana who gives it to her.

With ease, she steps into a lie that rolls expertly off her tongue.

And she blames us. The Leafborne.

She blames her own kind for what happened in the sky, and she praises Eldrion for vanquishing the threat.

That does not sit well inside me. Seeing her come to his aid like that doesn't feel right. And the way she looks at him afterwards doesn't either.

I try not to let myself think about what it means, but as I follow her and Briony towards the healing wing of the castle, I cannot help feeling like something is changing.

She is not the same girl I knew back in the Leafborne forest, or even the same girl who was sold at auction to a cruel fae lord. She's becoming something else, and I'm not sure I'm prepared for what that is.

As she moves, I study her.

I am not imagining it. Her mannerisms are the same, but they are a little sharper. Her voice, too, is different.

I want to shake her and tell her to come back to me. But I can't even touch her, let alone shake her.

She stops outside a large oak door and taps on it with her knuckles. It is Maura who steps outside.

"How are they? How is Raine? Is the baby—" Alana's eyes are wide, and her fingers are entwined in front of her.

Maura looks her up and down, then sighs heavily. "You are not welcome here," she says, turning away.

Alana catches her elbow. "Maura, please. We are kin."

"We are not kin." Maura draws her shoulders back and narrows her eyes at Alana. "We never have been."

I watch as Briony braces a hand on Alana's back, and Alana's wings droop. Her shoulders drop too, and the overwhelming, acidic taste of her rejection fills the air. Why must they always do this to her? Do they not see what they're doing?

With a flick of my own wings, I materialise in between Alana and Maura.

"There you are." Maura looks me up and down. "I wondered where you had gone, Kayan."

"You can see him?" Alana steps around me, looking at Maura.

"Of course, I can see him." She looks at me again, then shakes her head. "But I have nothing to say to him. I have more important things to deal with."

"Maura . . ." I try to catch her arm but, of course, can't take hold of her.

She shudders, a flicker of my energy zipping through her. "She is yours to deal with, now, Kayan. If you want to do what's right, you'll take her far away from here and drown her in a lake."

Briony releases an audible gasp. Alana turns away, clutching her stomach as if Maura's words have physically wounded her. Purple smoke begins to curl at her feet. Her shoulders stiffen. She spins back around, and her wings fly out to the sides, glowing with flickering purple light.

"See." Maura looks her up and down. "If she's not out of control now, she will be soon." She looks at me and holds my gaze. "Don't say I didn't warn you, Kayan."

❄

By THE TIME WE REACH ALANA'S CHAMBERS, SHE IS shaking from head to toe. Briony lingers in the corner of the room, watching us.

"How are you . . .?" she asks, her voice almost a whisper.

"He's been here for weeks," Alana says, pacing the room.

"You didn't tell me?" Briony sounds hurt.

"I thought you'd accuse me of losing my mind," she replies, casting a quick glance at me. "I'm not convinced that I'm not."

"Briony sees me too, Alana. So does Maura."

"How? I thought it was only me?" she asks, then shakes her head. "It doesn't matter. What matters is . . ." She hesitates, then glances at Briony. "I'm sorry. I need to talk to Kayan."

Briony smiles at her, although it's a sad smile. "I'll go and freshen up." She looks down at her clothes, laced with dust and some traces of blood.

When she closes the door behind her, Alana rushes towards me as if she wants to fall into my arms. She stops a few paces away, then lets out a frustrated growl.

"I'm sorry," she says. Tears are in her eyes. "I know you saw me with Eldrion and I'm sorry, Kayan."

"We don't need to talk about that."

"Yes, we do."

I shake my head, and sit down at the end of the bed. "No, we don't. What is happening between you and Eldrion is not important right now. What's important is whether you are all right?"

She studies me for a moment, then shakes her head and laughs. "All right? No, of course I'm not all right. Finn was lying to me. From the very day I met him, he was deceiving me. At least, I think he was. Unless his intentions were good and then they changed?" She is almost talking to herself. Her thoughts tumble from her lips, dancing around each other as she tries to piece together what has happened.

"There is no way to know what Finn planned or when he planned it, Alana. All we know is what he has done. Focus on that. His actions don't lie."

She meets my gaze, and I know she is thinking of Eldrion as well as Finn.

Both have done horrendous things. She loved Finn. Does she love Eldrion? Could she still love Finn after what she's witnessed?

If the answer is yes, I'm not sure I know her at all.

"What do we do now?" She sits down hard on the coffee table opposite the bed. "Do you know? Can you tell me?"

"I know I'm here to help you." I hang my head a little, sincerely wishing I could give her a better answer. "That's all I know, Alana."

"And how can you help me, Kayan?" She tilts her head, waiting for my answer. "What can you do to fight a demon when you cannot even touch?"

I breathe in deeply and pinch the bridge of my nose. My thoughts are racing. "I could help you track him?" The words form at the same time as the thought.

"Track him?"

"I tracked Rosalie." I try not to flinch as I say her name because the need to be closer to her is almost too much to bear.

"Rosalie?"

"I needed to know if she was all right."

"Is she?"

I hang my head. "No. She's not."

Alana rises from her seat and crosses the room towards me. She rests her hands on my legs, but I don't feel them and she doesn't feel me because she sighs a little and takes them back.

"She's living with the man who bought her at the auction. He is . . ." I trail off, combing my fingers through my hair. "I need to help her."

"We will." Alana meets my eyes. "I promise, Kayan. Help me find Finn, and when all this is over, I'll help you rescue Rosalie."

"You promise?"

She nods firmly. "I promise. Solemnly. With every breath. We won't leave her there, Kayan."

And there she is . . . the Alana I know. She's still there. Her warmth, and her kindness, and the sincerity in her eyes that has always made me feel so at home and so seen.

"Thank you." I reach out and touch her face. She leans into me even though she cannot feel me. "Thank you, Alana."

True to my word, I leave Alana and hover above the citadel, my ethereal form shimmering in the dimming light. The city below is eerily quiet, as if holding its breath in anticipation of the storm to come. I don't know if the Sunborne believed Alana's lie, but the fact the storm clouds are still gathered above the castle, and only the castle, makes me think they are still in hiding.

I close my eyes and try to focus. Searching for Rosalie was different. Her essence was familiar, and I had our memories, and our feelings for one another to draw me to her.

I wanted to find her, and while I want to help Alana, there is no part of me that truly wants to see Finn.

Ever again.

But if I want to help Rosalie and stop what's coming, I need to do this.

Perhaps this is my purpose.

I take a slow, shuddering breath and look towards the storm clouds.

An idea forms in my mind, and I fly towards them. They crackle with a dark energy that makes my translucent skin flicker with trepidation.

But his energy is here. I feel it.

Bracing myself, I move into the centre of the storm clouds.

Here, the energy is darker still. Colder. Trying to catch hold of it and tame it feels like I'm trying to grasp smoke with my bare hands.

I breathe it in and try to remember how it feels, then I drift lower, skimming the rooftops of Luminael.

As I near the outskirts of the city, I feel a faint pull. It's not Finn, not exactly, but something . . . adjacent. I follow the sensation, letting it guide me towards the shoreline.

The beach stretches out before me, pale sand growing darker as the sun dips below the horizon. I scan the area, looking for any sign of disturbance. That's when I spot it – a set of footprints leading towards a cluster of cliffs in the distance.

I follow the trail, moving faster now. The footprints lead to the mouth of a cave, barely visible in the shadow of the cliffs. As I approach, I feel a surge of energy – dark, pulsing, alive. This has to be it.

I pass through the cave entrance, the rock offering no resistance to my spectral form. The air inside is thick with moisture and something else . . . something that makes my non-existent skin shiver.

I drift deeper into the cave, following a winding passageway that seems to descend forever. Finally, I emerge into a vast underground chamber. At its centre lies a pool of water so dark it seems to absorb all light.

I hover at the edge of the pool, peering into its depths. There's something down there, I can feel it. But unlike with Rosalie's mansion, I can't simply will myself to the other side. Whatever magic protects this place, it affects even spirits like me.

But I do not need to go inside.

All I need to know is that this is where Finn has brought the Shadowkind.

And that something very bad is happening here.

FOURTEEN

Garratt

*E*very elf in the kingdom knows the secret ritual. The one that has been passed down from generation to generation. The things we are supposed to whisper, hunched over a cauldron of magic, like something from a fairy tale, to summon each other – warn each other – if evil approaches.

To my knowledge, it has only been used once: to rally the elves before the first Great War of our kind. When we battled forces that no longer exist, and when we were still considered noble and wise.

It has been so long since anyone saw us that way.

We are not abhorred like the Shadowkind, but we are not respected either. Elves have become something to laugh at. Jokers. Tradespeople. Merchants. We are the ones who swindle and steal in order to get by. Who double-cross, and play cards in taverns, and drown the memories of our greatness in ale.

But it is time, now, for us to remember who we were.

Elodie watches me closely as I pull back the trapdoor that leads to the basement below the inn. Don't get me wrong; I thought about running.

Every instinct in my cynical body told me to leave Pria, leave Elodie, run. Save myself. Flee the city and never look back because I'd be quicker and safer on my own.

But then I thought of my wife. I saw her as if she was standing right in front of me, and I saw the look of dismay on her face. Disappointment. *What have you become, Garratt?* She'd have whispered it to me. Not with malice but with sorrow.

And the thought of her voice sounding like that made me pull myself together and, against all my better instincts, take Pria and Elodie to the one place I've never shown anyone before.

Down in the basement, I head for the shelves at the back of the room. Pria follows me, and helps me move them aside to reveal a door. She raises an eyebrow at me, but doesn't speak. Elodie is lingering at the foot of the stairs. She seems petrified of her own shadow, and wants to be close to me and far away from me at the same time because I got her into this mess.

Looking at her now, shaky and clammy, I almost feel guilty for dragging her into my life. She and I were supposed to be nothing more than a bit of fun. I cared for her, and I told myself that made it okay for her to love me. I told myself I was giving her what I could, and that should be enough.

I hope she doesn't expect me to be the one to protect her in all this. Because I barely have the strength and fortitude to protect myself.

That's not who I am.

It might have been once.

But now, I look after myself.

As I open the door, and it groans loudly on its hinges, I realise that I'm not doing this because I feel it's the right thing to do. I'm doing it because the thought of my wife's disappointment is too much to bear.

And because if I run, where will I go?

That thing Finn turned into? He's not going to just set up camp in the castle and rule peacefully for the rest of his days. He wants destruction. And, no matter where I run or how far, his shadows will reach me.

Especially if he knows I betrayed him.

But there is safety in numbers. If the elves band together, we have a chance.

"What is this?" Pria folds her arms and stands back, examining the shrine in front of her.

It's more of an altar than a shrine, in actual fact.

Candles, symbols etched onto the wall, and a large silver bowl. Next to it, a silver jug.

"It's how we tell everyone that trouble is coming our way." I lift the jug. It is full to the top. Despite everything, this is the one tradition of my mother's I have always kept. Ensure the jug is full. Always. So that when you need it, it is there.

I exhale slowly and motion for Pria to step back.

She moves out of the way as Elodie moves forward. From the corner of my eye, I notice her try to take Pria's hand, but Pria scowls at her and shrugs her off.

Was Elodie always like this? A scared child with no gumption or wit about her?

I close my eyes and breathe in deeply, raising the jug.

As I pour the water into the bowl with one hand, I start to stir it with the other and begin to whisper the words I never thought I'd need to use . . .

"Vael'sor ith'mar, lun'dae kir'ath, Shal'mor fen'thi, rae'lum vor, Eth'nar sil'vai, dae'lith kun, Thae'sor vael'mar, lun'dae kir.

"Ith'rae shal'vor, eth'lum fen, Mor'vai thae'kun, dae'nar sil, Vael'lith sor'mar, lun'rae kir, Eth'mor shal'vai, dae'lum vor."

"What did you say?" Elodie whispers.

Part of me wants to tell her to be quiet. But a pang of guilt tugs at my gut, and I force myself to answer her.

"I said . . . Kin of starlight, heed my call, Through shadow and light, come to me, By ancient bonds and sacred vows, Gather now, from near and far.

"Time of need, time of change, Elven brothers, elven sisters, Unite our strength, unite our will, To face the darkness, to shape our fate."

"Oh," Elodie replies, biting her lower lip. "It sounded beautiful."

The water is turning blue. Dark at first, then brighter. It starts to glow. It swirls faster. A pattern forms on the surface. Elodie and Pria move closer. Then Elodie lets out a small gasp. It turns into a cry of pain.

She shakes her arm and looks down, pulling up her sleeve to examine her skin.

I do the same.

Pria stares at us.

On our forearms, a symbol is appearing. Red at first, like it is being drawn there, right now as we watch, by a red hot poker.

But then it settles and becomes blue, glowing like the water in the bowl.

It is a symbol I have never seen in the flesh, only ever in books and described by my mother. An intricate pattern of vines and branches unfurls across my skin, weaving together to form a perfect circle.

It burns viciously, and as the heat subsides, I expect the glow to darken too. Only, it does not. It keeps glowing. Shining into the gloom of the basement.

"What is it?" Elodie breathes.

"This will be happening to every elf in the kingdom right now," I tell her. "Your parents never warned you about it?"

She shakes her head. "My parents died when I was a baby. You know that, Garratt."

I did know that. But I'd forgotten because I've paid so little attention to anything she's ever said to me. "Well . . ." I put my hand on her shoulder, trying to offer a sliver of comfort. "Most of us know what it means. It means something bad is coming, and that it's time to come together. No elf can ignore the call."

"Come together where?" she asks, her voice barely a whisper.

"I'll show you."

WE GATHER ON THE OUTSKIRTS OF THE CITY. IT IS PITCH dark, and the lights of Luminael seem more dim than usual. Even the stars are hiding. Behind the thickening clouds that have been gathering all day.

"They all just came?" Pria gazes in amazement at the crowd in front of her. At least fifty of us, all with glowing tattoos on our forearms.

"They did." I am shocked, too. I didn't truly expect them to appear.

Many faces, I know from the tavern. But many, I don't. And I wonder whether elves throughout the kingdom are, this moment, making their way towards Luminael.

"You made the call?" asks an older elf with curly grey hair.

I nod at him. "I did. Pass the word. Trouble comes. We head to the library. There, I will explain."

He does not question me, just presses his lips together solemnly and whispers my words into the ear of the elf next to him.

When the truth has circulated, all stand silent. I look at the elf beside me and he holds out his arm. "They are wait-ing," he says. "They will follow you."

"No." I shake my head. "I am no leader. They should follow someone else."

"Many know the way," he says. "That is not the issue. The issue is that you summoned us, so you now lead us."

I glance at Elodie. She smiles encouragingly at me as if I should be pleased. But Pria purses her lips. Elodie might see me as some kind of loveable rogue, but Pria sees me for what I really am; a backstabbing con artist who serves only himself.

She knows I'm doing this to secure my own survival.

And she knows, because of that, I'll step forward and let them think of me as some kind of saviour.

I raise my arm. My tattoo glows brighter. From the back of the crowd, someone calls, "We follow."

The others echo, "We follow, we follow."

Then the man beside me tugs my sleeve. "Here," he says. "Take this" He offers me what looks like a staff. It's only when I examine it closely I realise it's one of two sticks he was using to help him walk.

When I take hold of it, however, my fingers grow warm. The tattoo seems to spread down my arm. Bright blue light swirling on my skin. It flows into the stick, down its ridges, then forms a glowing ball of light on the end of the stick.

I hold it high above my head and look up at it.

Everyone else looks at it, too.

Elodie whispers, "Cool . . . that's so cool."

But a sense of dread has settled deep in my stomach. "I am

not a leader. I was not meant to do this. Someone else should take charge."

"You made the call," the man repeats, staring at me with dark eyes. "So, you better be ready to do this, son. Because no one else can. You're in charge of these people now. So, you see them to safety."

As I move slowly through the crowd, it parts on either side of me. Pria puts her hand firmly on my shoulder. "Well, well, well," she says. "Looks like you got what you always wanted, Garratt."

I swallow forcefully but do not turn to look at her.

"These people trust you. Implicitly. Without you having to do anything to prove yourself. You're in charge."

"I have never wanted to be in charge of anything."

Pria rolls her eyes and scoffs at me. "Nonsense," she says. "You love controlling people, manipulating people. I've seen you playing your games. We all know what you're like."

"Games," I hiss. "Meaningless games. Scamming people to get a little extra money out of them. Twisting people against one another so I can sneak in and take advantage. Not this. Not . . ."

Shrugging, Pria withdraws her hand. "Well, maybe not. But this is what you've ended up with. So, you better pull yourself together."

I hold my breath in my chest, letting it swell and burn behind my ribs. I don't know why I'm doing this when everything inside me is telling me to run as fast as I can in the opposite direction.

But, despite my better judgement, I lift the staff high in the air and call, "Follow me. To the library on the shore."

WE WALK FOR HOURS. WHEN WE REACH THE SHORE, sunset is upon us and the beach is cast in an eerie almost-darkness. We approach on foot, on the sand, all fifty of us moving as one towards the place we'll be safe.

But then I feel it.

The darkness in the air.

I stop, and everyone else stops too.

"What is it?" Pria asks, hand going to the dagger on her waist as she peers into the distance.

"Something isn't right," I whisper.

I can see the outline of the caves from here. Silhouetted against the velvety night sky, they look completely unassuming.

I am still staring when the ground starts to rumble beneath my feet.

A crack appears on the beach. It stretches from between our crowded-together bodies all the way along the sand towards the cave. Another rumble. And then the beach begins to split open.

The crack becomes wider.

We jump back, scrambling to keep from falling.

It stops, about a foot wide, exposing nothing but inky blackness below the beach.

But the rumbling does not stop. Now, it sounds like feet. Feet and . . . wings.

"Garratt . . ." Elodie's voice cracks as she whispers my name. She grabs my arm and grips so hard I almost release a growl of pain.

I stare in the direction she is staring.

From the cave mouth, a swarm emerges.

A swarm of fae with huge black wings, and red eyes, and black veins on their pale skin. They keep coming and coming, so many of them, screaming into the air and coming and coming until the beach is barely visible anymore.

"Garratt . . ." Elodie shakes me. "What do we do?"

I look down at her, then I turn to the others, lift the staff high, and yell, "Run! Run now!"

FIFTEEN

Alana
_____

I can't sleep. It's impossible, and I don't know how anyone else can be sleeping either.

I have expected Eldrion to come and knock on my door. If not him, then Kayan. I thought he might have returned by now with news of Finn.

But he hasn't.

I am alone, as I was so many nights when I first arrived here.

Staring at my surroundings, it all seems so long ago now. And the woman who sat by the fireplace and allowed a jester to tend to her wounds seems like a different person. Someone I don't recognise.

What would she think of what I've become?

I pace up and down, simply unable to rest. It feels as though we are wasting time, and yet my body aches with the need to rest.

I look out of the window at the moonlit rooftops of Lumi-nael, visible beyond the citadel and the water that surrounds it. Above, obscured now by night, Finn's storm clouds still glare down at us. Watching. Promising something more, something darker, something we cannot stop.

I want to believe we can.

But deep down, it all feels futile. Afterall, I've seen it happen. So has Eldrion, and so far everything we saw has come to pass.

Despite everything, all of our actions simply led us straight to the outcome we were trying to prevent. We created Finn. We allowed him to become what he is now. If we had ignored the visions and done nothing, what then?

If Eldrion had never bought me at auction and dragged me here, or if he had never charged Finn with tracking me down, or if, or if, or if . . .

I let out a frustrated cry and slam my fist into the wall. It hurts. I am not as strong as Eldrion or as able to let the impact bounce straight off me. I rub my knuckles and glance at the door. Briony has not appeared either, and that makes me worried.

I thought she would come to update me on Raine and the baby. Of course, I care for Pen too. But the baby . . . I just can't stand the thought of anything happening to that baby.

From the beginning, it was a beacon of hope.

Watching her belly grow more rounded, and hearing her talk about her wishes and dreams for the tiny creature that had not yet made it into the world, gave us all something to cling on to.

If there was any doubt in my mind about what Finn has become, I only need to picture him standing over a pregnant, injured fae, and choosing to leave her and her baby to die. And then I remember he is lost to me.

Even Eldrion would not do that.

Would he?

I stride to the wardrobe and grab a long, thick shawl. I wrap it around myself to guard against the chill of the night, and leave my room.

It still feels so strange to be able to do that, and as I walk the halls of the castle, I expect to be stopped at any moment by a guard and dragged back kicking and screaming.

Instead, they look straight past me as if I am not really there at all.

Clearly, Eldrion has instructed them to leave me alone.

Noticing the tattered wings of a guard standing at the foot of the staircase that leads to Eldrion's chambers, I wonder why he is still here. Why are any of the Shadowkind still here? Surely, they sense that Eldrion's power has weakened?

Are they here out of loyalty? Or fear?

I hesitate at the base of the stairs. Thinking of him up there alone, everything in my body tells me to move towards him. But I ignore it.

I tear myself away from the promise of his touch and continue towards the healing quarters. In all truth, I do not know why Eldrion has such quarters in his castle. From what Briony told me when I first arrived, he was very reluctant to allow any of his servants or guards medical care even if they needed it.

That was precisely why Finn tended my wounds, and why Briony introduced me to him.

For a horrific moment, I find myself wondering – not for the first time today – whether I am still able to trust Briony. Everything in my heart wants to believe she is the friend she says she is. But what if I am wrong? I was wrong about Finn. What if she is a spy in our midst? What if she was part of his game all along?

When I reach Raine's hospital room, I shake the thoughts of Briony and her friendship from my head. I trust her. I have to. Because without her, I truly have no one.

I tap gently, but before I can push the door open, Maura appears.

Just the sight of her sends guilt and shame to the surface of my skin, enraging my cheeks until they blush furiously.

I sigh heavily and hang my head. Without making eye contact, I mutter, "Please. I just want to know how the baby is."

There is a long pause, and then Maura steps into the hall-way, closing the door behind her. "The baby lives, and so does Raine."

Relief floods my chest. "And Pen?"

"He will live, also."

I step back, bracing myself against the wall behind me. For the first time in days, I smile. A true, happy smile.

"Good news, isn't it?" Maura says.

When I look up, she is watching me carefully.

"Of course," I reply.

"It could have gone differently."

"I know."

Maura frowns, looking down at her hands. She has clasped them together in front of her stomach. When she looks back at me, her voice is a little softer. "Will you walk with me, Alana? I feel we need to talk."

Even though I know it is ridiculous, my heart lightens at the sound of her words. Less venomous, more maternal. "I'd like that," I tell her sincerely.

Side by side, quietly, we walk away from the healer's wing. We stop at a large open archway that looks out onto the castle courtyard. Cool air drifts in, kissing our faces.

Maura places one hand on the stone frame and exhales heavily. She doesn't turn to face me, just keeps looking out at the stillness in front of us. "I have an apology to make to you, Alana."

Again, my heart flutters.

"I have handled this badly. From when you were young, I got it wrong."

"Thank you," I breathe. "Thank you for saying that."

She does not react to my words, just carries on speaking. "I always knew what you were. I was there the night you were born, and I was there when the Lady of Luminael told your mother what she had done to you when you were still just a babe in the womb."

"You knew?"

Maura nods slowly.

"You should have told me."

"Yes," she says. "I should have told you, and I should never have spoken up for you when the rest of the village wanted you to leave."

I frown, trying to understand what she's saying because it sounds like an apology, but it also sounds like she's telling me she should have allowed me to be banished from the village.

This time, she does turn to me. "I should have explained it to you, and given you the chance to do the right thing."

"The right thing?"

"I should have given you the chance to end your own life and spare us all the misery you have brought upon us."

"Maura . . ." I step back, physically wounded by her words. "None of this is my fault." I am stuttering, barely able to speak because I'm afraid I will start to cry.

"It is all your fault," she sighs. And somehow, the lack of anger, and the amount of pure resignation in her words is what hurts the most.

"I . . ."

"You are no longer one of us." Maura stands firm and tall, her wings curling out sideways. "There are only three Leaf-borne fae remaining in this world. Four, once the baby is born."

"But . . ."

"You are not one of us," she repeats. "You are nothing to

us, and we are nothing to you. As soon as Raine and Pen are fit to leave this place, we will be leaving."

"But where will you go? Finn is still—"

"His fight is not with us. We will go somewhere we can be safe. Somewhere far away from you and your twisted games."

"I am not playing games. I did not do this!" Hurt turns to rage and flares on my skin in flickers of purple light.

The smoke is back. It drifts towards Maura's feet but she simply steps through it, turning her back on me.

"Maura . . . please," I call after her, but she does not look back. "Maura?" She still does not turn back. "Don't leave me alone. Please."

She disappears into the darkness at the end of the corridor. I hear Raine's bedroom door open, and close, and silence descends.

"Please . . ."

I storm into Eldrion's chambers without knocking. They are dark. There is no fire in the grate. Purple light still crackles on my skin, illuminating the walls in an eerie hue as I pass through the room I have stood in so many times before.

As if he was expecting me, he is sitting up in bed, a sheet across his waist, leaning forward onto his thighs. He looks up as I enter, and I storm towards him.

Dropping to my knees, I tug the sheet away from him, but he catches my hand and stops me. Holding my wrist, he stands slowly, towering above me, then makes me take his place on the bed.

"Open your legs," he commands, nudging my knee roughly with his own.

I do as he says, and he lifts my skirt.

I drop my shawl and lean back on my hands, spreading my thighs for him as he settles between them. Gently, he pushes my underwear to the side.

I expect his movements to be fast and hard and frantic like they have been so many times before, but this time, they are different.

He draws his tongue along my folds as if he has all the time in the world to make me come. A sigh parts my lips, followed by a small gasp of pleasure as he starts to suck my clit, pressing down on my stomach with the flat of his palm, grabbing my hip with his other hand.

As he touches and licks and sucks, I struggle to push the thoughts away that are racing in my mind. He stops. I look down at him, and he rises slowly.

"Your mind is elsewhere," he says, not in an accusatory tone, but with a strange level of affection that I would never have expected to hear.

"I need you to help me forget," I murmur.

Eldrion stares at me, then nods. He crosses the room, and returns with a band of silk he has pulled from his robe. He binds it around my eyes, taking away my sight. Then he pushes me down onto the bed, moving my body with ease, as if I weigh nothing at all, and settles between my legs.

Having my sight purposefully taken away is different from simply closing my eyes. It removes something; some element of control.

And this time, when he uses his tongue to tease my core, I am able to feel it. All of it. Every exquisite moment of it.

I wind my fingers into his hair and tilt my pelvis up, grinding into his mouth as my pleasure builds. Roughly, he pushes my legs back, exposing me even more. He holds them in place, and groans with approval at the sight of me.

"You taste so good, Alana," he mutters as he starts to suck again. More hungry this time, more desperate, as if he is trying to devour every morsel of my arousal.

I cry out and reach back to grab hold of the headboard.

And he does not stop. He keeps on teasing, and coaxing, and expertly manoeuvring my orgasm through my aching body until it settles exactly where it is supposed to be and starts to build. My legs tremble, my toes curl, and my cries turn into shuddering breaths.

I become completely silent, giving in to every simpering whisper of pleasure as it zips down my spine and makes my entire body convulse.

As my orgasm fades, I tug the blindfold from my face.

Eldrion looks up at me, and smiles.

It is more of a smirk, and it makes me want to slap him. But even as I want to push him away, I find myself reaching for him and pulling him up towards me.

He does not ask me to touch him or seem like he expects it. Instead, he positions himself behind me. I move away, but he wraps his arms around my waist and tugs me towards him. For a moment, I feel the burning need to get up and run. But then he kisses my shoulder, and yawns, and it feels so painfully normal and right and good that I yawn too.

I nudge backwards, and hold on to his arms as he curls around me.

I do not remember falling asleep. But I remember I felt the safest I had ever felt. And I remember feeling too tired to be guilty for it.

SIXTEEN

Rosalie
___

J sit at the ornate dressing table, staring blankly at my reflection. The woman looking back at me is a stranger – hollow-eyed, pale, sadness etched into every line of her face.

Is this really what I've become?

My fingers trace the edge of the drawer where I keep the torn pieces of Kayan's portrait. Even now, I can't bring myself to look at them. The pain is too raw, too fresh.

He is gone. The words echo in my mind, a cruel mantra that won't let me rest. Kayan is gone, and I never got to say goodbye.

I close my eyes, trying to block out the opulent bedroom that has become my gilded cage. Instead, I let my mind drift back to happier times, to the day Kayan first told me he loved me.

It was a warm summer afternoon, the kind where the air shimmers with heat. We were by the lake, our usual spot when we needed to escape the watchful eyes of the village. Kayan was skipping stones across the water's surface, each one jumping farther than the last.

"Show off," I teased, nudging him with my shoulder.

He turned to me, grinning that lopsided smile that always made my heart skip a beat. "Jealous of my superior stone-skipping skills?"

I rolled my eyes, trying to hide my smile. "Oh yes, I'm absolutely green with envy. However will I go on, knowing I can't skip a stone as far as the great Kayan?"

He laughed, the sound echoing across the water. Then, suddenly, his expression grew serious. He took my hand, his touch sending a jolt of electricity through me.

"Rosalie," he said, his voice soft. "There's something I need to tell you."

I remember the way my heart raced, the mix of excitement and fear that flooded through me. "What is it?"

He took a deep breath, his eyes never leaving mine. "I love you."

Three simple words, but they changed everything. I stood there, stunned, unable to speak.

Kayan's face fell, and he started to pull away. "I'm sorry, I shouldn't have—"

I cut him off, throwing my arms around him and kissing him with everything I had. When we finally broke apart, both breathless, I whispered, "I love you too."

The memory fades, and I'm back in the present, tears streaming down my face. I wipe them away angrily. What good are tears now? They won't bring Kayan back. They won't free me from this nightmare.

I stand abruptly, needing to move, to do something, anything to distract myself from the ache in my chest. I pace the room, my fingers trailing over the expensive furnishings. All of it meaningless, all of it a mockery of the life I should have had with Kayan.

A wave of fury washes over me. This isn't fair. None of this is fair. Kayan should be here, alive and well. We should be together, building a life. How did we go from dancing in the forest to this?

Fire blooms in my palms. For a moment, I'm tempted to let them grow, to watch as they consume this gilded prison.

But no. I can't. Not yet.

Because my husband is stronger than me, and he would not allow me to live if I tried to escape him.

I extinguish the flames, my resolve hardening. I will find a way out of here. I will make those responsible for Kayan's death pay. And I will honour his memory by living, and by fighting.

I walk to the window, looking out at the manicured gardens below.

"I miss you," I whisper, imagining Kayan standing beside me. "I miss you so much it hurts to breathe sometimes."

In my mind, I can almost hear his response. "Then breathe for both of us, Rose. Live for both of us."

I nod, squaring my shoulders. Yes, I will live. I will fight. And I will never, ever forget him.

A knock at the door startles me from my reverie. "My lady?" It's one of the servants, her voice timid. "Your husband requests your presence for dinner."

My husband. The word tastes like ash in my mouth. But I push down the revulsion, schooling my features into a mask of calm. "Tell him I'll be down shortly," I call back.

As I turn to my wardrobe to choose a suitable dress, I catch sight of myself in the mirror once more. This time, I see a flicker of something in my eyes. Determination, perhaps.

Or defiance.

As I wait for him to enter the dining room, I place my hands firmly in my lap and press my lips tightly together.

At dinner, he likes me to be a pliant, sweet-singing bird. He likes me to ask about his day, and offer oohs and ahhs when he tells me deathly boring details about the duties he has carried out on behalf of Lord Eldrion.

From what I can tell, this mostly involves watching over the lands that Eldrion's family gifted him many centuries ago, shouting at villagers, and occasionally fucking them.

He takes great delight in telling me about those exploits. The women he seduces, if one can call it a seduction when he wields so much power over them that they cannot refuse him for fear of retribution.

Tonight, he shall get none of these things from me. My lips will remain sealed. I will not utter a single word. Not a sound. My silence will be my protest against this life I have been doomed to live.

When he enters the room, stomach first, all bluster and red cheeks, the stench of ale comes with him. No doubt, he spent his afternoon in an elvish tavern completely unbefitting of a man of his standing.

There is only one reason to frequent the taverns.

As he draws closer, I realise he smells of sex, too, and it disgusts me.

He sits down in the chair at the head of the table, his large frame barely squeezing into the seat. He gives his wings a flutter and lets them drift out to either side of him. They are gold, like the other Sunborne in Luminael.

Only his look dirty and old.

Like him.

"Are you not going to greet your husband?" he barks.

I keep my eyes cast down to my plate, and do not move or speak.

A Shadowkind fae pours him a glass of wine. I hear him take a sip, smacking his lips together before leaning back in the chair with a creak that shudders in between my bones.

"I said, are you not going to greet your husband?" This time, he hisses the words like a curse.

I still refuse to look at him.

I am poured a glass of wine, too.

He bangs his fist on the table and my wine sloshes over the sides of my glass.

"You refuse to speak to me?" he asks, rising from his chair and striding over to stand behind me.

I had thought it would take a little longer to get him this worked up. Clearly, he is quicker to anger than I thought. But I do not back down. I cannot, not now.

A hand lands on my throat. Hard. He grips my neck and jerks my head backwards so I am looking at him upside down. From this comical angle, his moustache looks ridiculous.

I smile, and I know it makes me look as if I'm crazy, but I don't care.

"What the fuck are you laughing at?" he spits.

I close my eyes. He can't make me look at him.

With a shove, he lets me go and I jolt forward in my chair. He stays behind me. I feel the air moving as he beats his wings.

"You are losing your mind over your Leafborne boyfriend? Is that what's happening here?" He drools, lowering his mouth to my ear.

His breath lands, hot and sickly, on my cheek. And then a hand lands on my breast.

"You better pull yourself together and learn how to look happy by the end of the evening or—"

With a roar, I grab the knife from beside my plate and plunge it into the back of his hand. The one grabbing my chest.

It goes right through, grazing my own skin.

He yells and jerks backwards.

I rise from my chair and splay my arms out sideways. The candles flare. The room flickers with flame.

He looks me up and down, blood dripping from his hand, then he pulls the knife free. "You'll regret this."

He stalks towards me.

The candles blaze. Embers fall onto the tablecloth and it catches light.

But then he extinguishes them. One flick of his hand and they are all gone. And an invisible hand is around my throat now.

I stare at him as he comes for me. And when he lifts the knife to my throat, I smile.

SEVENTEEN

Finn

_____

"Why are we not going straight to Luminael?" Yarrow growls. He is pulsing with dark energy, longing to take back what is ours.

"We need to recruit a few more to our army first, Yarrow."

"Here?" He waves at our surroundings. "You think Mountainside fae will fight with us?"

"No, not here. This is just a nice little rest stop on the way. A chance for us to exercise our newfound strength. To test ourselves." I pat his back firmly. "Think of it as a training exercise."

"All right," he grumbles. "But then where do we find these extra recruits?"

"Of all the creatures in this kingdom," I say, raising an eyebrow at him, "who could be best persuaded with the promise of power, and money?"

"The elves?" Yarrow mumbles. "They're not fighters, Finn.

Good if you want some sacrificial fodder to go in the first wave, but—"

"Not the elves," I tut. "The Gloomweavers, Yarrow. We're going to recruit the Gloomweavers. And they are going to be delighted to finally have free rein with their cruelty."

Yarrow begins to smile. He nods approvingly. "Gloomweavers," he repeats. "Perfect."

"But for now . . ." I gesture to the trees ahead.

They are adorned with flags and ribbons. Pale pinks, and blues, and yellows, fluttering in the breeze. In the distance, music is playing. The sun is setting. How beautiful.

How sweet.

How wholesome.

Have we arrived in time for a celebration, perhaps?

We move through the forest as if we ourselves are made of shadow. We pass the villagers' cabins and their school and the place where they gather to eat and drink in the evenings.

And every single bit of it makes me sick to my stomach.

That they spent so many hundreds of years living like this while we, the Shadowkind, were bound and tortured and locked away. And it wasn't just the Mountainside fae. It was all of them. Every single sorry creature in this entire kingdom ignored our plight.

Because it did not suit them to see it, and it was not worth risking their own existence to help ease our suffering.

They are all ignorant, arrogant, despicable specimens. No better than Eldrion.

Because although it was his hand that did most of the damage, and his family who started our oppression, those who stand by and do nothing are just as complicit.

They just carried on living their lives. Having babies, playing with magic spells, fucking and dancing and living while we died slow, withering deaths behind Eldrion's walls. While our young were taken from their parents, and thrown into orphanages, wings bound, destined for a life of servitude to the ones who decided they were not good enough for anything else.

Not worthy.

Well, we are worthy now.

And we are about to show them what a mistake they made by casting us out and pretending we did not exist.

They will regret turning their eyes from our suffering.

As we approach the edge of the forest, I hear the roar of the ocean. We are near the cliffs. I turn to Yarrow, and his eyes flash in the gloom. "Take their eyes," I whisper to him. "But not until they have seen us and what we can do."

"Their eyes?" Yarrow's face sharpens into a grin that would send a shiver through any sane or normal being.

"They chose not to see us for centuries," I hiss. "Now they will have no choice. Take their eyes, but leave them alive."

Yarrow nods at me, still smiling, and then he spreads the word.

Murmurs of approval ripple through the trees.

We are not many, but we are powerful. And when we have shown our might, we will recruit more. The Gloomweavers will fight with us, and the elves too. Because elves are nothing if not whores for survival. At any cost.

I might take Garratt's eyes first, though. Because he really did betray me, and I really do not like that. At all.

When we reach the edge of the trees, I motion for everyone to stop.

We watch from the shadows as a crowd of Mountainside fae cheer and clap for a bride and her new husband. Their wrists are bound with pale yellow ribbons. They kiss, then the ribbons are untied, and they walk under an archway of their friends and families' wings.

They emerge smiling, elated. Music starts to play. The dancing begins.

And then we descend.

Yarrow takes the husband. I take the bride.

She screams delightfully as I wrap my arms around her waist and hold her tight against my body.

Yarrow holds the husband's head still.

I was not going to kill her. I intended to do exactly as I said: take their eyes and leave them alive and bleeding. But perhaps that is not enough.

If I learned one thing from Eldrion, it is that sometimes a display of might is necessary to make your audience understand what they are dealing with.

So, while Yarrow makes her husband watch, I take my

dagger from my belt and I slit the bride's throat. A long, clean line.

She coughs.

Blood spills onto her perfectly white dress.

I take her eyes next. She screams again, and the sound flutters down onto my skin like blossoms in spring.

I take a shuddering breath and let my wings fly wide.

The husband is screaming too. He tries to fight. He throws magic at me, but I bat it away with the flick of my wrist. And then I laugh because it is almost quaint that he thinks he might be able to overpower us.

Yarrow grins at me. "Now?" he asks.

"Now. The eyes." I inhale slowly. "And then do what you wish."

"Yes, my lord." Yarrow's voice is dark and dripping with blood lust. As he follows my command and leaves the new widower lying on the ground, scrambling to get away from him, I fly up above the trees and look down at the beauty I have created.

Shadows swirl and snake and choke.

Screams echo against the cliffs and drift up into the sky. Around me, my own shadows start to converge. They come to me and lift me up, and power vibrates in the air around me.

This is what we were destined to be.

We were destined to be the most powerful creatures in the kingdom.

And I cannot wait for Alana to see the world I am making for her.

As I think about her, something snags in the corner of my mind. A tingling sensation. Is she here? Is she watching me in her dreams?

I tip back my head and laugh, then swoop to the ground and pick up my dead, discarded bride. I lift her into my arms and walk to the edge of the cliff.

"Do you see, Alana? What we could be if we were together? What I am offering you?" I call into the ether, knowing, just knowing she can hear me.

"I am doing this for you! And you will be mine."

EIGHTEEN

Eldrion

OUR HUNDRED YEARS AGO

"RAYLON . . ." I JOG TO CATCH UP WITH MY BROTHER. MY wings flutter, lifting me a few inches from the ground and allowing me to tread pockets of air as if they are stepping stones.

He looks back over his shoulder and grins at me. "Keep up, little brother."

With a leap, he's taking off. Soaring into the air, his wings almost blocking out the sun, shining, light fluttering around their edges.

For a moment, I'm transfixed. He is two hundred years older than me and has, for my entire existence, been the thing I both admire and abhor.

I want to be him, but I hate what he is.

Because he is everything I'm not. He has powers I can only dream of and – arrogant bastard that he is – he delights in reminding me about it at every opportunity.

When we were younger, it didn't bother me as much; that's what older brothers did. They mocked, and teased, and helped you grow a thick skin. But now, with two hundred years of sibling camaraderie to look back on, I have grown to hate him a little.

A hate laced with love that is gradually, day by day, turning to spite.

If my mother knew the things I dreamed of in the dark, she would be appalled. She would disown me. For Raylon has been her golden boy since the day he was born. Almost literally. His hair is such a deep, luxurious shade of blond that when it catches the sunlight, it looks like a veil of gold.

And now he has her too.

Saera.

I loved her the moment I set eyes on her, and I knew I would never be able to have her.

She was brought to the castle by her parents and offered to my father as a peace-making gift – a way to forge an alliance between the Sunborne and the Desertborne fae.

My father said yes immediately without consulting Raylon or my mother.

Saera was given no choice, either.

I was there, in the shadows, watching as she stood with her head down, her eyes cast towards her pointed silver slippers, her hands clasped in front of her. She was pure innocence. A picture of beauty, and softness. Black hair, like the feathers of a raven, cascading down her back. Rose-red lips. And wings tipped with green; an earth fae.

She did not see me watching her, and I never revealed to her the way I felt that very first day she entered the castle. But Raylon knew.

When I stumbled back to our living quarters drunk that night and asked what he thought of his bride-to-be, he saw it in my face.

A look of recognition passed between us, and I saw his lip curl into a vicious smile.

He knew I loved her, and he knew he would do everything he could to flaunt her in front of me from that moment on.

Over the months that passed, I watched her from afar. Or, at least, I tried to. But it seemed as if, at every opportunity, she sought me out. She found me in the library, in the study, in the garden.

And then I started to seek her too.

She told me Raylon was not the sort of man she thought she would marry. "He's funny," she said, a note of hesitation in her voice. "But I don't think he's really interested in getting to know me." She paused and knitted her hands together in her lap.

In front of us, as the sun began to set, the ocean glimmered like a blanket of flames were dancing on its surface. She looked down at her feet dangling above the water that trickled out from the castle moat towards the sea.

"He is arrogant," she said, almost hesitantly, as if I might berate her for speaking badly of him.

I scoffed and rolled my eyes. "That's putting it kindly," I said. "But he has a right to be. He is powerful. More powerful than any other fae in the kingdom."

"Even more powerful than your parents?" she asked, her wings fluttering uncomfortably.

"Oh, yes." I nodded and leaned back onto my wings, using them like a cushion to allow me to relax backwards without falling. "Which is why they will give him anything he wants." I glanced at her, hesitating before adding, "What he wants is you."

A sigh swelled in her chest. "I know," she whispered. "But I want another."

And then our eyes met. The tip of her wing met mine. A shock like electricity ran through my entire body. Down my spine, through my limbs, into my fingers and toes.

My breath quivered in my chest.

I leaned towards her, already imagining the softness of her lips against mine.

And then I stopped.

I didn't say a word.

I left her there, eyes closed, waiting for me to kiss her, and I flew away. Back to the castle where I drank myself into oblivion, and continued to drink myself into oblivion every day until their wedding. And after.

Now, watching him fly away from me, I wish with every breath in my body that I had not turned away from her.

Not because I think we were destined to be together or that I would have loved her for the rest of eternity; now I know her better, I know she is too meek for my tastes. But because I wanted her and he did not.

Because he only took her to stop me having her.

Because if I hadn't let him see that glimmer of jealousy, he'd have discarded her and asked for someone else as a match.

Because I hate him, and to have her would be divine in its vengefulness.

It is in that moment I know I'm going to seduce my brother's wife.

"Wait for me, brother," I call, flying behind him, accepting his jibes and his cackling laugh as we soar above the city that belongs to him and only him.

"You will never be able to keep up with me, Eldrion. Just admit it." He laughs and spins so he's flying upside down, face tilted towards the sun like he's floating in a stream instead of on air.

I raise my hands, treading the air in front of him. "You've got me," I reply. "I will be forever in your shadow, big brother. No doubt about it."

The sun hangs low on the horizon as Raylon and I ride towards the distant settlement of Gloomweavers. As heirs to the lordship of Luminael, it is our duty to deal with them. His more than mine. But where he goes, I have always followed.

The journey has been long, the mood between us tense and uncomfortable. Raylon has been unusually quiet, his normally jovial demeanour replaced by a brooding silence that sets my nerves on edge.

As night falls, we set up camp in a small clearing. I busy myself with building a fire, trying to ignore the growing sense of unease in my gut. Raylon sits across from me, his gaze fixed on the flickering flames, his expression unreadable.

Finally, he speaks, his voice low and cold. "I know what you did, Eldrion. With Saera. With my wife."

The blood freezes in my veins. He knows? How?

"Raylon . . ." I start, but the words die on my lips. What can I say? How can I explain? Do I even want to explain?

He stands, his hand going to the hilt of his sword. "You slept with her, Eldrion. Your own brother's wife. The woman I love. How could you?"

I try to bite back the urge to scoff at him. He never loved her. He only chose her because he knew I wanted her.

"I'm sorry," I whisper, trying to feign repentance. "I never meant for this to happen. It was a mistake, a moment of weakness. I . . ."

"A mistake?" Raylon's laugh is harsh and bitter. "You've always wanted what was mine, haven't you? My birthright, my power . . . and now my wife. You're not fit to be Lord of Luminael. You're weak. Pathetic. No better than the Shadowkind that serve our meals and clean our stables."

I stand up, my wings flicking out to the side.

He laughs again. He thinks so little of me that it doesn't even occur to him I would fight him. Or dare to stand up to him.

In that moment, as he laughs at me, something in me snaps. All the years of resentment, of living in his shadow, of being the second son, come boiling to the surface. And with it, my shadow magic, usually so carefully controlled, bursts forth in a surge of uncontrollable rage.

Dark tendrils lash out, wrapping around Raylon's throat. He claws at them, his eyes wide, his lips helplessly trying to form my name.

I stare at him, yanking him to his feet and holding him hovering in front of me, the shadows gripping tighter and tighter around his throat.

I watch, as if from a distance, as the life is squeezed from him.

It is over in moments.

Raylon falls to the ground, lifeless, the shadows receding from his bruised neck. I stand there, shaking, staring at what I've done.

I've killed him. My own brother.

He is dead because of me.

I wait for guilt to crash over me, brace myself for the tidal wave of self-hatred, and the fear, and the loathing.

But it does not come.

Instead, I feel calm.

He is gone. And now, nothing stands in the way of me and Saera.

I will inherit everything that belonged to him, including her. And I will never have to hear his arrogant laugh ever again.

With calm, unshaking hands, I prepare a pyre for Raylon's body. I will tell our parents, our people, that he fell in battle against the Gloomweavers. That he died a hero's death.

They will never know the truth.

For a moment, as the flames consume Raylon's body, I wonder whether my mother might have foreseen this. Perhaps that was why she hated me all these years; because she knew what I would become.

But I shift the thought from my mind as quickly as it comes.

If she does know, she will not tell. For that would cause her to lose two sons, and she would be to blame for not having stopped me when she had the chance.

I stand and watch until my brother is completely gone.

I wait for the embers to die down, and then I walk through his ashes and leave him there. Nothing more than dust, now.

Gone. Forever.

I DON'T OPEN MY EYES. MY HEART IS POUNDING A VICIOUS beat against the inside of my ribcage. My body vibrates, but not with pleasure. It is throbbing with adrenaline, and guilt, and power.

I picture Saera. Her beautiful face. I remember the excitement I felt when I comforted her after Raylon's memorial service. And then I remember the hatred in her eyes when she looked at me.

"I know what you did," she spat at me. "We all know. And you should know that I will never allow you to touch me, Eldrion. Never."

Her words echo in my mind.

Never.

Never.

But then the absence of my power hits me like a tsunami.

The place where the shadows lived is empty. The place that swirled, and screamed, and undulated with the intense, overwhelming power that I was able to wield over almost everything. Shadows, light, dark.

It is empty now.

A cavernous void in which my inadequacies echo and amplify.

I see my brother's face.

I hear his voice in my head.

Beside me, Alana is warm and soft and I reach for her in the darkness. My fingers find her waist and trace their way up the curve of her body, over her hip, her stomach, until they find her breasts.

Following my fingers, my wing curls over, pushing the sheets away from her body and pulling her closer. Wrapping her up as if she is mine and will always be mine.

She releases a low murmur and wriggles back against me. The curve of her ass presses against my cock. Already hard and trying to resist the urge to slide inside her before she wakes, I press my lips to her neck, kiss the spot below her ear that makes her sigh with pleasure, and whisper, "I want to make you come again, Alana. I need to hear the sounds you make when I touch you."

She turns to face me, cocooned in the embrace of my wings. She strokes my face as if she is truly pleased to have opened her eyes and found me beside her.

"I don't know what you mean," she whispers. "I am always very quiet when you touch me."

She smiles. A playfully delicious smile that makes me want to flip her onto her back and thrust inside her right now. This second.

"You most definitely are not." I move the tip of my wing slowly down her throat, drawing a line down her neck, between her breasts, over her stomach.

She sighs and arches up into my touch. While my wings caress her, stroking her skin, leaving trails of pleasure over her arms, her breasts, her hips, her waist, I part her legs with my hand and rest my palm on her waiting core.

She is warm and waiting for me. Her legs open a little wider, and she turns towards me, remaining on her back, tucking one arm underneath the pillow, lying back as if she's ready to just close her eyes and let me pleasure her forever, and ever, and ever.

I cannot stop myself from kissing her. But this time, it is not a kiss filled with fury and fight. It is gentle, searching, an unspoken string of words and whispers that make her moan into my mouth and hook her arms around my neck.

She strokes my hair from my face, and opens her eyes, fixing her gaze on mine as I find her clit and press one purposeful finger against it. She nods, biting her lower lip, and tilts her pelvis so she leans into my touch.

I keep my finger still, applying pressure, the same pressure, watching her skin flush and her eyes widen. She stops biting her lip and releases a quivering breath. Her freckles look darker, and her eyes brighter.

When I finally move my finger through her wetness, slowly, she tilts her head back and sighs.

I reach her entrance and pause. "One finger? Or two?"

She looks at me, her entire body alive with pleasure. "Just one at first. Then two."

I smile. She'll get three.

As I thrust them inside her, the surprise on her face makes my cock throb with pleasure. Her eyes flash as if she's angry with me, but then they soften into the same playfulness I saw a moment ago, and she thrusts down onto the three large fingers that are now settled inside her.

I move them in and out, slowly. "You're so tight," I murmur. "But so very wet for me, Alana."

She fixes her eyes on mine, and I realise she is slipping her hand further beneath the sheets. She keeps staring at me while she curls her hand around my cock. Then she pauses, lifts her palm, spits into it, and returns it to my shaft.

Fuck.

The way she did that.

The complete dichotomy between the way she looks right now – soft and angelic and innocent – and the way she so expertly moistened her palm for my cock makes me moan. "Harder," I whisper, increasing the speed of my fingers in her pussy. "Harder and faster."

For a microsecond, she obeys me. But then she stops, takes her hand away, and sits up. Her wings flutter. She climbs on top of me and slides straight onto my waiting cock. She leans back, using her wings to cushion herself, and moves one hand to her clit and the other to her nipple.

I tuck my hands behind my head, lie back, and watch her use me as a plaything.

She rides me, eyes closed, moving to her own rhythm, making herself moan and whimper. And when her orgasm starts to build, I resist the urge to grab her hips or flip her over or tug her towards me so I can pull her breast into my mouth.

I bite down on my own pleasure and watch her.

Her eyes fly open and she catches my gaze.

"Don't come for me," I tell her. "Come for you. Whenever you want, however you want."

"Oh, fuck." Alana scrapes her fingers through her hair with one hand while the other furiously works her clit.

The pleasure building in my core is almost unbearable. But I cannot come until she does.

I am about to lose my ability to hold back when she finally explodes with pleasure. She cries out, her body stiffens, and then she goes completely silent. She closes her eyes, quivering on top of me for a long moment.

Then she falls forward, kisses me, and lets me thrust up into her deliciously wet cunt until I explode.

NINETEEN

Alana

I bolt upright, a scream caught in my throat.

Somehow, Eldrion and I fell asleep in each other's arms. But this sleep was different. It was not a comforting sleep; it brought with it the one thing I have been trying to avoid.

And now the vision clings to me like a second skin, refusing to fade even as I blink into the darkness of Eldrion's bedroom.

Is it because we are so close to each other that this keeps happening? That both of us keep slipping into visions we cannot escape or control?

My heart pounds so hard I feel like it might burst from my chest.

"What is it?" Eldrion's voice is sharp, instantly alert. He's already sitting up, muscles tense, ready for a fight.

"Finn," I choke out. "I saw him. He's . . . he's slaughtering the Mountainside fae. Taking their eyes. Turning more Shadowkind into demons."

Eldrion's jaw clenches, his eyes flashing with barely contained rage. "We knew he intended to turn the Shadowkind but . . ." He inhales sharply. Does he feel sorry for the Mountainside fae?

Is that what I see in his eyes?

"We have to stop him," I say, my voice stronger now, fuelled by desperation. "Eldrion, we have to do something. We have wasted time." I leap out of the bed and pull his robe around me.

Instead of making plans, we allowed ourselves to sleep and fuck and pretend we had all the time in the world.

"With what army, Alana, are we supposed to fight him? Most of the Shadowkind who remained loyal have fled. The Sunborne don't trust me anymore. And I'm—" he cuts himself off, frustration evident in every line of his body.

"Then what?" I snap, anger flaring hot and bright inside me. "We just sit here and let him slaughter innocent people? Then let him come for us?"

"Of course not," Eldrion growls. He slams his fist against the wall, leaving a dent in the stone.

"What if we play him at his own game. Trick him here and take back your powers?"

"He has an army of fae who can control the shadows now, Alana. I'm not sure my power would make any difference."

"So, you're just giving up? You're done?" I march over to

him and shake him. My powers are crackling beneath my skin. "Maybe I should go alone. Face Finn myself."

Eldrion rises up in front of me, his eyes blazing. "You are not a stupid girl, Alana, so do not act like one."

"At least I'd be doing something!" I shout, purple light flaring around my hands.

"And get yourself killed in the process?" Eldrion's voice rises to match mine. "What good would that do?"

"Well, it seems like we're all going to die pretty soon. Might as well get it over with. Seeing as you're out of ideas."

We glare at each other, the air between us charged with tension and unspoken fears. Finally, I deflate, the fight draining out of me. "What are we going to do?" I whisper.

Eldrion sighs. For a moment, I think he might be about to reach out and hold me. But, of course, he doesn't.

Instead, he pulls on his clothes and starts to pace the room. He pours himself a whisky and leaves the bedroom.

I follow him, and find him standing by the fireplace. Just like he did when he first brought me to his chambers and spent hour upon hour questioning me about my past, the Leafborne, and my powers.

"The Sunborne are our only chance," he says. "We need to persuade them to fight with us."

"Why should we need to persuade them? Will they not want to protect their city?"

"Sunborne fae are powerful," Eldrion replies solemnly. "But it has been many years since they had to fight for themselves or for anything else. They may feel it's safer to flee."

"Then we have to make them stay."

Eldrion nods, rubbing his jaw thoughtfully. "They want a banquet. They want to feel as if everything is normal. We invite them here tomorrow night. All of them. And then we'll make our plea."

"You think that will work?"

"If I tell them my magic is gone, maybe." He draws in a deep breath.

"You want them to know that?"

He shakes his head. "No. I do not, but I don't see another way. They are the most powerful weapon we have. If they decide to fight, we could stop Finn before he gets anywhere near the city."

Eldrion offers me the whisky glass and I take a sip. It makes my throat burn.

"He said he was doing it for me." I look down into the glass, my voice barely audible. "That he was offering me something. That I would be his."

To my surprise, Eldrion's hand lands firmly on mine. "You're not his," he says, his voice laced with venom.

"Then whose am I?" The question leaves my lips before I have time to think about it.

When I turn to look at him, Eldrion's jaw twitches.

"You belong to no one but yourself, Alana Leafborne. And don't let anyone tell you otherwise."

TWENTY

Alana
———

"*A*lana! Are you in there?" Fists are pounding on Eldrion's door. He rushes to open it, and I follow behind.

"You have to come. Now." Briony stands in the doorway panting, her hair coming free from its ties. "Both of you. The elves are here."

"Garratt . . ." Eldrion practically spits his name and draws himself up to his full height.

"Not just Garratt." Briony bites her lower lip. "He has others with him. Looks like every elf in Luminael."

"This is good." I stride forward and I'm about to take Eldrion's arm when I stop myself. We are not that to each other. I don't know what we are, but we are not in a place where we should be touching each other in front of other people. Even if the person is Briony.

"How is this good?" he growls, striding towards the door.

"We need larger numbers. The elves could—"

"We do not need elves on our side."

"You are being stubborn. Because Garratt double-crossed you, you're going to let them walk away without trying to make them join the fight."

"We do not need elves to fight with us. Have you ever met an elf?" Eldrion snaps, striding through the castle as though there is a fire at his heels.

Ignoring him, I turn to Briony. "What do they want? Why are they here?"

"Garratt seems to be leading them," Briony says. "But he won't speak to anyone except Lord Eldrion."

We emerge in the courtyard. It is sunny beyond the castle, but those same ominous clouds still haunt us overhead.

"What is this?" Eldrion splays out his wings, fluttering them so that their faded colour is not noticeable.

Gathered around the outskirts of the courtyard, the Shadowkind guards have hemmed in the elves.

They stand in a close-knit group. Maybe fifty of them of varying ages, all with the same slightly pointed ears and short stature.

"You dare to show your face here?" Eldrion marches towards Garratt. He is holding what looks like a staff. It glows blue in the soft morning light.

Garratt draws in a shaky breath. His hair is sticking up in tufts and he looks older than when I last saw him. Beside him, taller than the rest, a Shadowkind I recognise.

"Pria? You stand with them now?" Eldrion glares at the

Shadowkind, and as she moves forward, I catch sight of her guard's armour.

"I stand with whoever offers me the greatest chance of survival," she says matter-of-factly.

Beside her, Garratt rolls his eyes and a dark-haired elf standing to the other side of him tuts loudly.

"I should end you right here, right now," Eldrion says, moving closer to Garratt as the other elves stand back out of his way.

"Perhaps," Garratt says, holding up his palms. "But first, there is something you should know."

"I have heard that before, and look where it got us," Eldrion barks.

Before he can say anything else, I step in. "What is it you need to tell us?"

Eldrion glances at me, his eyes simmering with displeasure, but he folds his wings back and nods at Garratt to speak.

"We know where he is and what he is doing. We saw him." Garratt looks over his shoulder and the others nod and mmm in unison.

"Finn?" My heart starts to hammer hard in my chest. "You know where he is?"

Garratt turns his attention to me, sensing that I'm the more receptive out of the pair of us. "We were trying to get somewhere safe. We went to the library." His eyes dart to Eldrion, who growls deep in his throat. "Finn was there. But he wasn't him."

"We know what he is," I snap. "Tell us what he was doing."

"I don't know how to describe it." Garratt shakes his head. His complexion has paled. He swallows hard and tugs at his collar. He looks at Pria, and she rolls her eyes slightly.

"He has turned the other Shadowkind," she says. "They came tumbling out of the cave looking just like him. Bigger, badder, huge black wings. Shadows swarming around them."

"How do we know you're telling the truth?" I ask.

But then, at my side, I hear Kayan's voice. "*I saw it too, Alana.*"

I cannot see him, but I can hear him.

"*I did as you asked. I tracked Finn, and I saw it too. I felt the darkness in the cave and I waited. I saw what the elves saw, and I saw them running. They are telling the truth.*"

"We ran," the dark-haired elf says, echoing Kayan's words. She has tucked her arm through Garratt's. He squeezes her hand. "We ran as fast as we could, and we came here because we wanted to warn you."

"That is not why you came here," Eldrion speaks slowly.

"Elodie, be quiet," Garratt hisses at his female companion.

"It is, of course it is. I mean, yes, we hoped you'd help us. But mainly we wanted you to know what was happening. So you can stop it."

Eldrion narrows his eyes at her. Garratt looks like he wishes he was anywhere but here. Some leader he turned out to be.

"You have passed on your news. Now you may leave." Eldrion turns and moves back towards the large oak doors at the front of the castle.

"Leave?" I look from Garratt to Eldrion. "They can't leave." I turn back to Garratt. "You can't leave. We need all the help we can get to fight Finn." I cast my gaze over the huddle of elves. "Will you fight with us? Help us protect the city from him?"

A hushed murmur spreads through them. No one speaks loud enough to be heard, but it is clear what their answer is.

"Actually, I think Lord Eldrion is right." Garratt nods and starts to back away. "We should leave. We are no use to you."

"All right, then if you're going to leave, you could be our messengers." I walk to the front of the crowd. "You don't have to stay in the city. This is a fae matter, not an elvish one. But if you could reach the outer settlements. The Mountainside fae and the Waterweavers, and tell them what is happening, ask them to come to our aid . . ."

Garratt is shaking his head still. He holds up his hands again. "I'm sorry, no," he says. "Lord Eldrion got it right. We are no use to you."

As the elves begin to retreat, Pria steps away from them, lingering in the middle of the courtyard as if she doesn't know which path to choose. Does she stay and hope it is safer behind Eldrion's walls? Or leave with the cowardly elves?

They are at the archway when an uncontrollable burst of anger flares in my gut. It rages like an inferno beneath my skin. Unexpected but not unwelcome, because it seems I am the only one who is actually trying to prevent this kingdom from falling to the ash and ruin I have seen in my visions.

"You may not leave!" I shout. My voice echoes off the courtyard walls. Everyone is staring at me. "You may not leave unless you agree to help us."

There is a quivering pause. But I do not have the gravitas that Eldrion possesses. Someone sniggers at the back of the group.

I bite my lower lip, anger turning to rage in the pit of my stomach.

"Alana, calm down."

Kayan's voice, usually calming, feels nothing but patronising. And instead of settling me, it simply enrages me even more.

Why will no one listen to me?

"And you're going to stop us how?" the dark-haired elf, Elodie, snipes, folding her arms and tapping her foot. She reminds me of the girls who taunted me when I was growing up. The disrespect in her tone jogs a memory. More than one memory. A hoard of them, barrelling into the back of my skull.

I see Maura's face, and the faces of all those who have ever betrayed me.

I spin around, stride towards Eldrion, and grab the dagger from his waist. My heart is racing, beating a savage rhythm I cannot ignore.

I curl my fingers around the hilt of his blade. The one I know he keeps there because I feel it every time we embrace.

Eldrion does not stop me as I stride forward and grab the dark-haired elf by the shoulders, yanking her towards me. He tilts his head in curiosity.

And with him watching me, I feel stronger.

Elodie shrieks, and tries to fight me, but my magic is already binding her to me. Her back is pressed to my chest. My smoke creeps up her legs and around her waist.

I tighten my fingers around her neck.

"Alana, what are you doing?" Briony has rushed to my side. "Stop."

But I will not stop; Eldrion taught me this trick. He taught me that sometimes a show of power is necessary.

And if he will not do it, then I will.

I raise the blade to her throat.

"All right, we'll help you." Garratt rushes forward. Others agree, begging me to leave her alone.

But Garratt is too late. My blade has sliced open his girl-friend's throat.

I meet his gaze and tower above him, still holding her against me as her blood drips down the front of her clothes and her body goes limp in my grasp. "You're right," I tell him. "You will help us."

TWENTY-ONE

Kayan

The elf's eyes are still open. She has a beautiful face. Small, and round, with big green eyes that stare up at the darkening sky, reflecting the gathering storm clouds.

Her neck is open like a mouth with no teeth. Red, gaping, dribbling dark red blood onto the cobblestones.

Alana is breathing hard and fast. Her chest rises and falls. Her hand shakes, but she does not drop the knife.

She looks up and sees me standing above Elodie's body. She meets my eyes, but does not speak to me. Garratt drops to his knees beside Elodie. His hands hover above her body, then he slams his hand onto her throat and tries to hold it closed. The blood seeps between his fingers, coating them red. He presses his other hand on top of that one, but the blood is still coming.

It is in Elodie's hair now, making it darker and thicker. It's on Garratt's shirt, too.

"Do something." He looks at Eldrion. "Do something."

Eldrion is stock-still, like a statue, completely unmoving. His wings don't even twitch. Through their tips, the sun glints and casts strange pale freckles of light on Elodie's porcelain face.

Alana still hasn't spoken. She flexes her fingers on the knife's handle.

Pria looks from Alana to Eldrion but says nothing. Then, slowly, she bends down and hooks her arm under Garratt's, easing him to his feet. "She's gone," she whispers.

Garratt tugs against her, then meets her eyes.

"She's dead, Garratt." Pria nods at him. "She's dead."

Garratt pinches the bridge of his nose. He's shaking. He stumbles backwards, staring at the dagger in Alana's hand.

"Alana, what have you done?" I whisper.

She tilts her head, blinking at me. For a fraction of a second, panic crosses her face. Panic chased by guilt. But then it is gone. She narrows her eyes at Garratt, then clicks her fingers. His mouth drops open, and a plume of purple smoke bursts from his lips. It spirals into the air and swirls round, and round, then dissipates.

Pria steadies him. Garratt frowns and shakes his head. He looks down at Elodie. "I . . . I don't understand."

"I took her life, and I took your pain." Alana stalks towards him. I step between them, but she passes through me as if she doesn't see me anymore. When she reaches Garratt, a ring of purple smoke coils around his throat and holds him still for her. Pria steps away. Alana raises her blade.

Eldrion says nothing.

"Alana . . ." I tug at her arm, but of course she feels nothing.

She hears me, I know she does, but she is choosing not to listen.

"I eased your pain for you, Garratt," she says. Her voice is like poison and ice.

"Yes," he mutters.

"But I can give it back again, tenfold. I can make it hurt so much you wish you were dead." She snaps her fingers. The smoke around his throat creeps up towards his mouth. He slams his lips closed and tries desperately to hold them shut, but the smoke prises them open and makes him gag, and choke, and cough as it multiplies on his tongue and surges down his throat.

He drops to his knees. Elodie's blood coats his hands. He skids on it, sits up, scrambles backwards. He's sobbing. Tears stream down his face. He clutches his chest and starts to wail.

"Does it hurt?" Alana asks.

"Please," he murmurs. "Take it away again. Please."

She smiles. It is a smile that sends chills through me. It can't be real. This can't be Alana. Something has happened to her. Finn. Or Eldrion. They've done something to her, they've taken her powers and turned them against her. They've addled her brain.

"Do you see now?" Maura's voice makes me turn around. She is standing behind me, arms hanging loose at her sides, despair on her face. "Do you see what she is?"

When I turn back, Alana has, once again, relieved Garratt of his grief. He stands up, nodding, thanking her.

She smiles and tells him he's welcome. As if she just did him a favour. "I think I made my point. Did I not?"

Garratt nods, even though I don't think he knows what her point was at all; I don't think he knows his own mind anymore.

"You help us, we'll help you." She clasps Garratt's hand tightly. "That's a fair exchange, isn't it?"

Pria is standing behind Garratt, eyes wide, looking absolutely terrified.

But Garratt simply nods again. "Yes," he says. "A fair exchange."

"And if you don't help us . . ." Alana flies up so she's hovering above the crowd. "You know what will happen." She looks at Eldrion. Without needing to exchange a single word, he understands what she wants him to do. He scoops Elodie into his arms and flies so he is treading air beside Alana. He holds out Elodie's body.

Alana pulls balls of purple light into her palms. And then, while Eldrion holds Elodie still, Alana sets fire to her dead body.

The purple flames flicker.

Eldrion keeps holding her as if he doesn't even feel them. And then he lets her fall.

She hits the ground, the way I did, and her broken body is consumed by Alana's fire.

While she is still smouldering, the stench of charred flesh filling the air, Alana returns to the ground and stalks back towards the castle. "Follow," she calls.

The elves do not look at one another.

They do as she commands.

I CANNOT STAY HERE. I DON'T UNDERSTAND WHAT JUST happened and I don't know how to stop seeing it when I close my eyes.

So, I flee to Rosalie.

I feel her before I see her. Her aura is so strong, so beautiful, so calming that I almost forget what I just saw.

I find her by the fountain. She is sitting on the rim.

She trails her finger in the water, a look of melancholy contentment settling on her beautiful face. Her blond hair is pinned up, fastened at the base of her neck. A few gently curled strands have escaped to frame her soft, round face.

But there is something on her neck . . . Finger marks.

And there are bruises on her chest, and another on her cheek.

Biting her lower lip, she closes her eyes.

A wave of sickening realisation washes over me. He did this to her. He hurt her. Part of me knew that was what he was capable of, but seeing the evidence of it on her perfect skin makes me feel as though I can't breathe.

Even though I am not, in fact, breathing at all, because I am not here.

I stare into her face.

Oh, how I wish I knew what she was thinking, so I knew whether I could show myself to her or not.

I want it more than anything.

Especially now. I want to take comfort in her gaze, and her words, and her. But how can I do that when there is a chance that seeing me will break her?

While I watch her, she hooks her legs up and lowers her feet into the water. She doesn't lift her dress, just lets it dangle into the fountain.

It becomes damp, water seeping up through the fibres of the skirt so it clings to her legs, her knees, her thighs.

I am transfixed by her.

I cannot stop watching.

She shivers a little, and as I sit down beside her, still keeping myself invisible, I breathe warmth into the water.

She sighs, and a smile parts her lips. She moves her feet gently through the water, then she looks up at the pale moon and the velvet sky.

"I miss you, Kayan," she breathes. "I miss you so much."

Hearing her name sends an exquisitely violent shudder down my spine. Fuck.

I stand up, standing in the water, then kneel in front of her. I want to kiss her so badly my entire body aches with need. But I can't; she wouldn't feel it.

She will feel this though . . .

With water clinging to my fingers, I reach out, slip my hand beneath her skirt, and trail one slow line up her calf towards the back of her knee.

As the warmth and the wetness moves over her skin, her eyes widen. Her toes curl a little, and she instinctively leans into my touch. I add more fingers, stroking her again from her ankle up to her knee.

I know she loves this spot. This is where I would kiss when I was trying to drive her wild. I'd flip her over, watch her wiggle her perfectly round ass at me. I'd nibble her ass cheeks, the backs of her thighs, her hips. Then I'd use my tongue to tease this exact spot.

As I make circles with my fingers, she closes her eyes and tilts her head back. Her hand goes to her chest, and she strokes her collarbones, her breath quickening.

Her dress is tied at the front, gathered over her breasts, accentuating them, teasing me with the thought of pulling the string that will expose them for me.

I remember their fullness, her pale nipples, and the way they seemed to grow darker when she was aroused.

With my other hand, I nudge her legs open.

She can't feel me, but she obeys me anyway, and then, as if she's picturing me in front of her, she hitches her dress up around her waist.

A growl rumbles deep in my throat. It's so vicious I'm surprised she doesn't hear it.

I lick my lips as she lowers her hand to her core and starts to gently play with herself. She is circling her clit, breathing hard, chest shaking, when I push two fingers inside her.

I can't feel her, but I can imagine how she feels, and that's almost enough.

She can't feel me either, and yet her eyes fly open and she gasps, tilting her pelvis as if she's trying to take my fingers deeper inside her.

With her spare hand, finally, she tugs on the string that holds her dress closed over her breasts. The tie loosens, and she eases them free.

I look up at her, drinking in the fullness of her body. Fuck, I want to taste her. It's not enough just to feel her.

Kneeling up, my fingers still inside her, I seal my lips over her nipple. It peaks between my lips and when I start to suck, Rosalie whimpers.

Can she feel me?

"Fuck," she whispers. "Oh, fuck."

She is using three fingers now, making harder faster circles between her legs. I keep sucking, licking, teasing as if this were real and we were together.

A moan parts her lips, louder this time, and she reaches back to free her hair.

It cascades over her shoulders.

Fuck, she's beautiful.

And she's going to come.

I would know that change in her breath anywhere, and it drives me wild with hunger for her.

Standing up, I free my cock and wrap my hand around it. I might not be able to feel her, but I can feel myself.

I tighten my grip, watching her eyes roll back and her deep, steady breathing turn to a quivering panting that drives me wild.

I remember what it was like to have her lips on me, her hand around me, her throat taking me deeper and deeper.

And when she mutters my name the second time, I can't hold back. A shuddering orgasm sweeps through my entire body. I shudder and shout her name, and behind me, the fountain splutters viciously.

Rosalie comes too.

Her cheeks flush, her back arches, she parts her legs wider and grips the side of the fountain with her free hand. As it subsides, leaving her trembling, she opens her eyes and looks down at her body.

She frowns.

I follow her gaze.

Across her chest, the faintest of blue marks, glowing.

As Rosalie leaves me to return to her chambers, I sit where she sat and stare into the water. I need to get her out of here, and I can't trust Alana to help me.

The Alana I knew is fading, and I don't know if I can return and watch her disappear in front of my eyes.

I know why it is happening; she has been betrayed one too

many times, and mistreated one too many times. But that does not mean I condone it.

What she just did . . .

My mind returns to the image of the elf lying on the ground.

She killed someone.

For the first time, Alana hurt someone on purpose. Deliberately. With clear intent. She ended a life for what?

For the same reason Eldrion ended mine. A display of strength. An attempt to wield power over those around her.

And I cannot see how she can come back from that, now that the ice has started to form in her heart.

I am still thinking about Alana, my thoughts flitting between the way she dragged her blade across Elodie's throat, and the bruises on Rosalie's beautiful neck, when I hear movement in the distance.

I look up to see Rosalie's husband staggering towards me.

He pauses when he reaches the fountain and drops his pants, peeing into the water and sighing with relief.

He turns and looks up at Rosalie's window. Her lantern still burns. He smirks, adjusts himself in his pants, and sits down on the edge of the basin.

I stand in front of him.

He takes a cigar from his pocket and lights it. When he holds it between his teeth and starts to puff, he shakes his head and laughs. He looks down at his hand. There is a mark on top of it. He mutters, "Little bitch. She hasn't paid nearly enough of a price for what she did."

He stands, cigar still in his mouth, and looks again at Rosalie's room.

I am still in front of him but he is looking straight through me.

He moves forward.

And in that second, I know what I have to do.

I stretch out my arms and summon every ounce of magic in my veins. The fountain stops, the water moves in the wrong direction.

Rosalie's husband turns to look at it. "What the fuck?" He drops his cigar.

The water surges forward, curls around him, pushes and pulls, and drags him into the basin. Head first. It holds him down, his lower half kicking and struggling.

I do not move.

My magic keeps holding him. His breath shudders in his chest.

Still, I do not move.

Finally, he is still.

He's no longer breathing.

I stagger backwards.

He is no longer breathing. I killed him. Like Eldrion killed me, like Alana killed the elf.

Except, I did this for Rosalie. To protect her. The man I killed was evil.

I am not like them.

I am not like them.

TWENTY-TWO

Eldrion

*a*s Alana strides back into the castle, I follow her in a daze.

I am in awe of her, and yet I am terrified by what she is becoming.

It happened so suddenly, and yet it was not surprising. I saw the first flashes of it when she pushed Maura to the ground in the forest. And last night, when she came to me with hurt and humiliation and rejection simmering on her skin.

Watching her take the elf's life, an act I have carried out myself on more than one occasion, was like watching a younger version of myself.

Except, she does not seem to be struggling with it the way I did.

She is completely calm. At ease. As if she is completely confident that what she did was necessary.

I watch the sway of her hips as she walks, the way she holds her head high, the way she pushes open the doors to the entrance hall and strides inside as if this is her home now and not mine.

She doesn't just believe that what she did was right; she enjoyed it.

"Pria!" I shout for her. She comes running to my side. "Go with Marcus."

Marcus, who was waiting at the foot of the stairs, marches over and waits for my command. "Take the elves to the dungeon. Seal them in. I will deal with them in the morning."

Pria swallows hard.

"Can I trust you to return to the fold of the castle, Pria? Or do I need to lock you up, too?"

She shakes her head, standing straight and firm. "You can trust me, my lord. If you promise me safety, I promise you loyalty."

"You have yourself a deal," I tell her.

As the elves are hoarded off by Marcus, Pria, and the guards, I follow Alana. She is partway down the corridor, storming towards the chambers I now think of as ours when I grab hold of her wrist.

She spins around, eyes flashing purple.

She bites her lip at me.

Without speaking, I drag her into the shadow of the doorway and slam her up against the wall. She reaches for my pants, frees my painfully hard cock, and parts her legs.

I slam up into her without pausing to touch her or kiss her or tease her into wanting me. She already wants me. She wants the release I can offer her by fucking her until she screams my name.

Tilting her head back, she cries out, then pulls her dress down and frees her breasts. I take one in my mouth, biting her nipple, then sucking it hard.

She grips the back of my head, holding it in place as I fuck her.

Then she slides her hand down between us and begins to circle her clit.

She comes hard and fast, and she does not wait for me to come too.

Instead, she pushes me away, stands back, and says, "Finish yourself. Show me how much I turn you on, Lord Eldrion."

Her eyes flash again. Her breasts are still free and naked. Her face is flushed. She slips a hand under her dress and begins to play with herself.

I wrap my hand around my shaft, feeling both completely exposed and completely unable to resist her. When I come for her, she comes too.

Then she pulls her dress up, smooths her hair, and leaves me to clean myself up.

TWENTY-THREE

Alana
———

I stride towards the edge of the rooftop, my hands gripping the stone balustrade. The breeze does little to soothe the fire burning within me, the rage and desperation that seem to consume every rational thought in my head.

My body still vibrates with pleasure.

I enjoyed it.

Did I?

Did I enjoy taking her life?

I close my eyes and picture Elodie's face. The way her skin broke open as I sliced through it, and the glint of her thick, silver blood as it trickled down her throat onto the stone below her breathless body.

I did that. I ended her, and I didn't use my magic to do it. I didn't need magic. Which surely means I am so much more than they think I am?

Even Eldrion didn't see it coming. He would never have expected me to do it. He was shocked. But he was also turned on; the way he fucked me proves that.

Behind me, I hear his footsteps, slow and measured. "Alana," he says, his voice barely audible over the wind. "We need to talk. You took it too far."

I whirl around, my eyes blazing. "What do we need to talk about? Finn has an army of shadows at his command, an entire legion of darkness that will stop at nothing to see us all destroyed. And you stood there, doing nothing, willing to let them walk away."

He takes a step towards me, his hands held out in a placating gesture. "I was not going to let them walk away. I was going to—"

"What?" I square up to him, power quivering beneath my skin.

I adore the way he is looking at me right now, as if he wants to tame me and worship me at the same time.

He shakes his head and looks away from me. "Trust me," he says. "It's a slippery slope. Once you begin the slide into darkness, it's very hard to claw your way back."

"You would know." I follow him to the edge of the roof and look down on the citadel.

"Yes," he says, turning to me. "I would."

I press my lips together, holding in the anger that flutters in my heart when I look at him and think of Kayan.

Kayan, who was so appalled by me that he has vanished. Perhaps never to return.

"It is done now." I fold my arms in front of my stomach. "There is no use wishing I could take it back."

He turns to me and cups my face in his hand. "Do you wish that?" he asks, studying my face.

I inhale slowly, holding the breath in my lungs for longer than usual before shaking my head. "No," I say firmly. "I do not. It worked, didn't it?"

Eldrion lets go of me and scrapes his fingers through his hair. "It did," he says. "But you acted on impulse. It may not have done."

"Everything you've done was calculated?" I ask, my thoughts returning to Kayan.

"Everything," he replies. "Every evil thing I have done has been the result of careful consideration."

I frown at him. A laugh swells in my chest. "I think that's worse." I smile. I can't help it. "Choosing those things after weighing your options . . . having the chance not to do them and then doing them anyway? That's—"

"What being a ruler means." He draws back his shoulders, and for the first time in days, I see him as he was. Without his fading wings and his lack of power. Lord of Luminael. All powerful. "It means making hard decisions. Something you'll have to get used to if you're going to take my place."

"Take your place?"

Eldrion shrugs. "You have power, Alana. I don't. It's gone. It makes sense that you would be the one to rule if I cannot."

For a moment, just one fleeting moment, a pang of sympathy settles over me. But then it is gone.

And in its place, I feel . . . excitement.

ONE HUNDRED YEARS AGO

"It's beautiful." I stand on the sheepskin rug, staring at the fire in the grate.

"Rosalie helped me." Kayan slips his arms around my waist. The fire crackles orange, and white, and blue, and green, and purple. As it dances, little shapes rise up, formed from the flames themselves. Roses, hearts, birds, trees.

"She's amazing." I press my palms to his hands, leaning back into his chest, my wings pressed between us.

I could stay like this forever, soaking up his warmth; I have never felt as calm as I do around him.

"She's certainly got tricks up her sleeve," he chuckles. "But I feel sorry for Bryant."

"Why?" I laugh, spinning around and looking up at Kayan. He is taller than me by almost a foot, and from here, his blond hair looks darker.

"She's very demanding, let's put it that way," he says. "High energy."

"And I'm not high energy?" I quirk an eyebrow at him.

He runs his thumb over my lips and smiles. "No. You're stillness, and sweetness, and everything that's calm."

There's that word again. Calm.

I sigh and reach up on the tips of my toes to kiss him. We have never been alone like this before. Perhaps because we knew what it would lead to.

I hook my arms around his neck and press myself against him. As the kiss deepens, his hands roam my back, then skim my wings, pausing to tease their lower tips.

I sigh, a moan parting my lips, and tilt my pelvis towards him.

When I feel him stiffening beneath my touch, I smile into his lips, and he laughs. "I'm sorry," he says. "That's not what tonight is about. I just wanted time. The two of us. After everything, I thought you might just want to be alone. To talk."

I shake my head, staring into his eyes. "Talking is the last thing I want to do, Kayan."

My hands go to his waist, and I unfasten his pants.

He swallows forcefully, closing his eyes and sighing as I push them down over his hips, then slip my hand into his underwear. We have touched like this before, but never somewhere like this.

Never completely alone, locked away from the world, able to go as far as we want to go.

As I start to touch him, he groans and tugs open the front of my dress, his lips finding my nipples and taking them, in turn, into his warm, waiting mouth. He sucks, and nibbles, and then I sink down to the floor and kneel in front of him.

Staring at me, he strokes the side of my face, tucking my hair behind my ear. "You don't have to . . ." he whispers.

But I'm already smiling up at him, opening my mouth, running my lips and tongue along his shaft.

The noises he makes, and the way his wings unfurl and fill the room, glowing blue, energy pulsing, makes me moan, too.

I love turning him on like this. The power I feel over him. It's almost intoxicating.

As I take him deeper into my mouth, and hold onto the backs of his thighs, I close my eyes, and wonder . . .

What if I could make him want me more?

It feels so good when he touches me. What if I could intensify that feeling for him? Make it bigger, and more intense?

I search for his feelings, fingers of curiosity snaking out from my mind to his. If he feels them enter him, he doesn't betray it. His stance doesn't change, and the noises he's making don't change.

He is lost in the moment, enjoying every second of my touch.

I don't need to do this.

But I don't get to play with my powers the way the others do.

I glance at the fireplace.

I don't get to make beautiful shapes out of water and fire. I don't get to coax leaves from the trees or flowers from the ground.

All I am told to do is squash my power down, rein it in, soften it, dampen it.

I stand up, take his hand, and tell him to lie down. When he does, I remove my dress. It falls to the floor and he stares up at me as if he can't believe I am here and that I'm giving myself to him.

When I lower myself onto him, and he fills me up, I lean back and his hands drift up my stomach, to my breasts.

My hair falls over my shoulders. He teases its ends.

I let my wings free, the way his were, and they flutter as the pleasure builds inside me. And the entire time, I continue searching for him.

Finally, there it is. Shockwaves of pleasure are pulsing inside his skull and in the air around him. I can see them behind my closed eyes. I can feel them.

I latch on to them and breathe in slowly, concentrating on trying to make them bigger, and brighter, and louder.

Kayan moans loudly. "Oh my stars, Alana. Fuck. What are you doing to me?"

The pleasure dripping from his voice drives me wild. So, I focus harder. I pull, and tease, and curl tendrils of pleasure inside his mind until he is writhing beneath me, and then I am dragging it inside me and letting it bleed into my own pleasure, amplifying, dancing beneath my skin until there is no telling whose is whose anymore.

But then.

Then I feel something else.

Not his pleasure.

His power.

I falter. Kayan's hips change rhythm beneath me and his breath slows. His power is there. I can see it. I can feel it. Blue energy, pulsing, and pulsing, and pulsing.

It is so beautiful.

I want to feel it the way I feel his arousal. I want to capture it, just for a second, and know what it feels like to have elemental strength inside me.

I tip my head back, my lips parting as a loud cry flies from them and swells in the room around us.

I have it.

His magic. Behind my eyes, blue bolts of light flood my body. They trickle through my veins, and wind themselves around my ribs, and take hold of my heart.

They grip tighter, and tighter, and my breath becomes shallow.

I open my eyes.

I can barely see. Blue light fills the room, swirling in the air between us, around us.

The fire is no longer alive. Only electric blue light, like waves, twirling faster and faster. I press my palms onto Kayan's chest. His power and his pleasure combine and explode like a volcano of liquid heat inside me. Trembling, barely able to breathe, I stop moving and look down at him, searching for his eyes, desperate to see if he felt the way I did.

But his eyes are still.

His body is stiff.

Dark blue lines cover his chest and arms, and beneath him, his wings are no longer blue. They are grey now.

I fall sideways and stumble to my feet. "Kayan?" I whisper, standing, unable to move, staring down at his lifeless body. "Kayan?"

What have I done?

TWENTY-FOUR

Rosalie

I wake to the sound of urgent knocking. For a moment, I'm disoriented, and all I can think about is how much my ribs hurt, and the bruises that circle my throat.

The knocking comes again, more insistent this time.

"Come in," I call, my voice still hoarse from where he choked it from me.

The door opens, and Mira, one of the younger servants, bursts in. Her face is flushed, her eyes wide. "My lady," she gasps, "you must come quickly. There's news."

"What is it? What's happened?"

Mira's excitement seems to bubble over. "It's Lord Cassius, my lady. He's . . . he's dead."

I frown at her. Dead? My husband, the man who bought me at auction, who kept me prisoner . . . dead?

A laugh bursts free from my lips. "Dead?"

Mira nods. She is wringing her hands together in front of her stomach. "Dead," she repeats after me.

"How?" I manage to ask, my mind reeling, trying to swallow down the bubble of laugher that just doesn't seem to want to go away.

"An accident, they say. He was in the garden, drunk after visiting the taverns in the city. He fell into the fountain and drowned."

"He drowned?" I walk to the window and pull open the shutters. I am staring at the fountain, half expecting his body to still be lying there. "In the fountain?"

Mira approaches me and puts a gentle hand on my shoulder. I flinch at her touch, because my entire body is still bruised and aching. "I can leave," I whisper. "This means I can leave?"

Mira's eyes are shining. "You could, but that's not all, my lady. If you stay, you've inherited everything. The estate, the wealth, all of it."

I stare at her, unable to process what she's saying. "That's . . . that's not possible. Surely there are other relatives, or . . ."

Mira shakes her head emphatically. "No, my lady. Lord Cassius had no living relatives. And you were his wife. It's all yours now."

This can't be real. It has to be some kind of trick, or test. "The other nobles won't allow it," I say. "They'll find a way to take it all away. They won't let a woman he purchased at auction inherit his wealth."

To my surprise, Mira's smile only grows wider. "That's just it, my lady. We've already spoken to the staff, and everyone is behind you. We'll support you in taking over the household. No one else needs to know the . . . circumstances of your marriage. Cassius didn't tell anyone. He didn't want them to know he couldn't get himself a wife through his charm and charisma."

"They think I married him for love?" There's that laugh again, bursting free from my chest.

My mind is racing. Freedom is within my grasp, but can I trust it? After everything I've been through, it seems too good to be true.

"Why?" I ask, turning to Mira. "Why would you all support me?"

Mira's expression softens. "Because you've been kind to us, my lady. Even in your own suffering, you've shown us compassion. That's more than Lord Cassius ever did."

I sink into a chair, overwhelmed. Memories flood my mind – of Kayan, of Alana, of the life I had before.

I could go back to it.

Except, I couldn't. They were sold, too. Our home no longer exists. But now, suddenly, I have the power to change things. I could find them all, rescue them, bring them here to live with me or take us back to the forest. Make a new home. A safe home.

"What happens now?" I ask, my voice barely above a whisper.

"Now, my lady, you take your rightful place as the head of this household." Mira's voice is firm, confident. "We'll help you. You'll need to make some public appearances, of course, to establish your position. But behind closed doors, you'll be free to do as you wish."

Free. The word echoes in my mind, tantalising and terrifying all at once.

I stand up, squaring my shoulders. "Very well," I say, surprised by the strength in my voice. "Let's begin."

TWENTY-FIVE

Alana

———

"They are coming?" I am staring down at the courtyard. From here, I swear I can still see the remnants of the elf's blood staining the cobblestones.

Her body was removed sometime in the night.

I try to think about the elves, locked away in the dungeon the way we were when we first arrived here. I try to make myself feel sorry for them, but it is as if something in my heart has turned to ice.

Where there was too much feeling and too much hurt, and so many years of betrayal after betrayal, there is now nothing but a soothing coolness that spreads from my chest, down my arms, to my stomach.

Even moving feels easier, as if I've somehow become lighter overnight. I woke expecting to feel the oppressive thrum of guilt between my ribs. Instead, I feel powerful.

Eldrion sips his whisky and watches me. The way he watches me is changing. He seems curious, impressed, but also a little nervous. Perhaps because he suddenly feels like he cannot predict what I will do next.

"Do you want to talk about what happened?" he asks.

I shake my head, and enjoy the sensation of my hair falling down my bare back. I am naked in front of him – done with the pretence of wearing robes to seem coy. We have fucked too many times for that now.

"What is there to talk about?"

"You took a life, Alana. And I assume it was the first."

I turn slowly and observe Eldrion's expression change. He looks down into his drink, and a sigh makes his fading wings shudder a little.

"The first is always the most difficult."

"It wasn't difficult." I sit down in his armchair and cross one leg over the other.

He quirks an eyebrow at me. "Alana, you can't just turn off your feelings."

I frown at him, search my body for emotion, and then tilt my head. "Except, maybe I can. Maybe that has been my power all along. The ability to switch off my emotions so I can do what needs to be done." I uncross my legs, deliberately giving him a view between them, before crossing them again. "You have tried over the years, and you've done a good job of it. But perhaps you didn't go far enough. Perhaps that was the problem."

"Alana . . ." He stalks across the room and stands in front of me, arms folded. "Don't get me wrong, this version of you? It's hot as hell. Watching you step into your power is something I will never tire of. But I know you. You are your feelings, and they don't just disappear at the click of your fingers."

"You're wrong."

"You're protecting yourself. You're shutting down because it's all too painful."

"Does it matter?" I snap, my words clipped and sharp. I look up at him, eyes flashing, magic blooming in my upturned palms. "Does it really matter? If it saves us, does it matter if I lose myself a little on the way?"

"Yes," he says, nudging my knee with his own. "Because right now I'm not sure what we're trying to save, are you?"

I frown at him. Something soft and uncomfortable is forming in my chest. I bite down on it until it solidifies and darkens. Slate, now. Not butter or honey or something easily pliable.

"We are trying to save the kingdom from Finn and his army."

Eldrion nods slowly. "Yes," he says, looking me up and down, his eyes lingering on my nipples. "That is what we are trying to do."

"In which case," I flutter my eyelashes at him, "why are we still discussing one dead elf?"

I watch as Eldrion grits his teeth, then leans forward and kisses me. His hand settles between my legs. "I'm not sure," he says. "I'm really not sure."

I sigh and lean back, but then I remember what we were discussing and I grab his hand, stopping the sensation of overwhelming pleasure from growing any more intense. "Are they coming to the castle tonight?"

He takes back his hand and stands up. "They're coming."

"All of them?"

"I summoned every Sunborne in the city. They are all coming."

I exhale loudly. "Good, because I don't know how much time we have." I reach up and take his whisky glass, drinking down a large sip and, this time, enjoying the burn in my throat.

I close my eyes, and a flash of Elodie's face, and her throat, and the cobblestones enters my head. I push it away and push down the softness.

"Alana . . ." Eldrion sees it. I know he does.

I stand and push past him. "I'm going to get dressed, then we should summon the guards. I assume you have some kind of defence plans for the castle? But most of these guards are new. You lost a lot of your old ones when they left with Finn and the other Shadowkind. You should—"

He strides over to me and takes my elbow roughly, pinching it between his thumb and forefinger. "I like seeing you taking control," he says. "But remember, this is still my city, Alana. My people. My kingdom. You are not in charge here."

I shake my head, a wry laugh making my shoulders stiffen. Of course. He has been doing nothing more than humouring me. Letting me play war games, and enjoying the torment I'm suffering for trying to help him.

He has distracted me with the feelings he coaxes from my body, but when it comes down to it, he is no different from the rest.

He does not respect me, or admire me, or believe I am truly capable of anything.

He sees me as a weak-willed female, unravelling in front of him.

He wants me to give in to my emotions because then I will not be able to step into the strength that's inside me. He will regret underestimating me.

"I apologise," I say tightly. "I got carried away."

Eldrion's brow creases suspiciously. He puts his hand on my hip and tugs me a little closer. "Don't apologise," he says. "Just remember I'm the one making decisions." His grip tightens. "And don't kill anyone again without my permission."

As his lips crash into mine, and my body comes alive under his touch, that word burrows into my psyche.

Permission?

Oh, hell, no.

I don't need his permission. He has no magic. He needs me if he ever wants a chance of seeing his magic again.

I will show him exactly what I'm capable of. And he will be sorry. They will all be sorry.

When the Sunborne begin to filter in through the archway into the courtyard, I watch them cross the place where I took Elodie's life, and I try to feel anything but a sense of rigid determination about what I'm going to do next.

Their feet gently meet the ground where she lay, and where her blood drained from her lifeless body.

And I feel nothing.

They all look so regal. Glittering, gossamer wings. Long, flowing robes, and an air of serene contentment – the kind of contentment that comes with knowing you are one of the most powerful beings in the kingdom.

My magic flickers in my hands.

I think I am starting to understand what that feels like. After tonight, I will know for sure. And no one will ever be able to tell me again that I am nothing or that I would be better off dead.

I will not need to rely on anyone but myself. I will save them, and they will be grateful.

Behind me, the door opens and closes softly. Briony is looking at me differently from the way she did a few days ago. Seeing me end Elodie's life changed something in our friendship, but she will see it was for the best. I'll make her see that.

"They're arriving," she says, bowing into a small curtsey the way she does for Eldrion.

"You don't need to talk to me like that." I turn around and stride over to her, wrapping my arms tightly around her smaller frame and hugging her closely.

She is stiff and awkward in my arms, and a flash of irritation burns beneath my skin. When I step back from her, I know my cheeks are flushed.

"Something is the matter?"

Briony looks away from me and shakes her head. Her dark hair falls down over her shoulders. She's not wearing her old uniform, but a pair of riding pants and a tunic. Leather boots, as if she's preparing to leave at any moment.

"Briony?" I speak her name a little more roughly than I intended to.

She looks up, moistening her lips by pressing them together. "I'm worried about you, Alana." She wrings her hands together in front of her stomach.

I have never seen her as weak before, but in this moment, I am starting to, and it draws a sense of deep irritation from deep inside me.

"You do not need to worry about me."

"I haven't seen you like this before. The Alana I know would never . . ." She hesitates, meeting my eyes as if she's searching for something. "You would never have . . ."

I meet her gaze with stony indifference. "You are trying to persuade me to feel guilty for what I did."

"I'm not trying to persuade you, Alana. I am trying to understand why you don't. How you could have so quickly changed into . . ." She gestures to me, and shakes her head again.

"Into what?"

"Him." She holds my gaze. I don't know if she's talking about Eldrion or Finn or both. It doesn't really matter which; she is wrong. And she has proved she doesn't know me at all.

"The reason I don't feel guilty, Briony, is because I have no more guilt left to feel." I pace away from her back towards the window. The Sunborne are gone now, inside the castle, and the sun is setting. "I've spent a lifetime feeling guilt, and pain, and sorrow. I have hated myself for so long, I don't remember whether I ever saw myself as anything but wrong or broken."

"I am so sorry you felt that way." Briony hurries over to me and puts her hand on my arm. I feel a flash of warmth towards her, and the soft part of me that keeps trying to make me pay attention to it whispers, *trust her, lean into her, let her comfort you.*

"Your people treated you badly. Maura's words hurt you." She moves in front of me and looks up into my eyes. "I know she spoke to you the night before you hurt Elodie."

She can't even say the word killed.

"I heard what she said. I was with Raine in her room, and I listened from the shadows. She is awful, and the things she said were awful. But you are not what she said you were. You have done nothing wrong, Alana."

"I killed someone." I speak with a firm, matter-of-fact tone, even though tears are clamouring at the back of my throat now. "I killed someone, Briony." My voice turns to a whisper.

I blink back tears. Her hand strokes my arm.

I tug out of her grasp and stride over to Eldrion's armchair. Sitting down, I tilt back my head and close my eyes.

I cannot do this. If I let in the grief, and the fear, I will not be able to do what needs to be done.

"Alana, please." Briony kneels in front of me. She places her hands on my knees. "Come back to me." She smiles, and everything inside me wants to trust her.

But how can I?

The only person I can trust now is myself.

"Can we talk more tonight?" I ask her, trying to bring softness to my tone.

Briony nods and squeezes my knee. "Of course," she says. "I am here whenever you need me." She stands and reaches out to stroke my hair. "I'm your friend, Alana. We have been through too much to stop trusting each other now."

I lean into her touch. It feels like my mother's used to. But she betrayed me too – by leaving me in a world that hated me without the tools to fight back.

"Thank you." I take Briony's hand and squeeze it. "I couldn't do this without you. I really couldn't."

"You'll dress for dinner and come to join us?" she asks, gesturing to the gown Eldrion had someone hang up for me by the fireplace.

It is long, and silver, and perfect.

"I'll be down in a moment."

At the door, Briony stops and smiles at me over her shoulder. "It's going to be okay, Alana. With the power of the Sunborne behind us, Finn doesn't stand a chance."

She disappears through the doorway, and I walk over to the dress. I trail my index finger over its silky fabric. "He really doesn't," I whisper. "He really doesn't."

TWENTY-SIX

Briony

*K*ayan is waiting for me in the hallway. I am still not used to seeing him, but I have stopped questioning it. I have stopped questioning anything anymore.

"Did you speak to her?" he asks, following me as I hurry down the hall towards the noise and movement of the Sunborne, gathering for what they think is another of Eldrion's feasts.

"I think I got through to her." I sigh with relief. She listened to me, she let me hug her, she let down the wall she'd put up. "I think it's going to be okay."

"We need to get her away from Eldrion," Kayan says. "Being around him is changing her."

"It's not just him." I stop and fold my arms. "Maura was cruel to her, she said terrible things. You should make her apologise. It would mean a lot. All Alana wants is to be accepted."

"Maura will never . . ."

"She might if she realised what her cruelty is doing."

Kayan shakes his head. His blond curls fall over his face, and he sighs deeply. Watching him is a strange experience. His body is the same, but it is also not the same. It glows a little, sometimes more, sometimes less.

"I will try to speak to her," he says. "But she is old and stubborn. I cannot see that my words will make any difference."

"Try." I resist the urge to squeeze his arm because I'm not sure what it will feel like, or if it will feel like anything at all.

"You're a good friend to her," he says as we move once more towards the grand hall.

"As are you," I tell him. "To still stand by her even though she is in love with Eldrion. After what he did to you . . ."

"In love with him?" Kayan's tone changes. He shakes his head. "She is not in love with him."

"I believe she is. And I believe he loves her, too. Have you not seen the way they look at each other?"

Kayan frowns. "That's not possible. Eldrion is . . ."

"I'm not saying it's a good thing." A small shudder grips my shoulders. "It's the kind of love that seems like it could destroy the world if they let it grow too big."

"Isn't destroying the world what we're trying to prevent?" Kayan asks. We have reached the large oak doors that lead into the dining hall.

"Precisely. Which is why we need to do everything we can to remind Alana who she really is, and where she comes from, and that this life here in this castle is not what she's fighting for."

Kayan presses his lips together. He nods slowly. "I'll talk to Maura."

"Alana promised me we could talk later. Bring Maura to her chambers. If we can just get them to work together, and undo all the hurt, maybe . . ." I sigh and pinch the bridge of my nose. I'm not sure I believe what I'm saying. Maybe I'm being naive. Is it really possible to come back from what Alana did?

"We have to try," Kayan says, as if he's reading my mind. "We owe it to her."

I nod and thank him. "Yes, we do." Then I push open the doors and enter at the back of the hall.

While Kayan goes to find Maura, I position myself at the rear of the dining hall with the other Shadowkind who remain in the castle.

Most are guards, but there are a scattering of others, too.

Observing them, I wonder whether I still feel like one of them. For so long, we had a joint enemy, and a shared experience. But now I seem to stand apart from them. Although they could have run, they did not. I did, but I returned free. They are still bound to Eldrion. They could leave if they wanted to; he could not stop them now. But a lifetime of being sealed behind these walls has made them unable to make that choice.

They will be here to the bitter end.

Whatever that looks like.

As the music begins to play, the same music Finn entered to every night when he performed his acrobatics for the Sunborne's entertainment, the crowd quiets.

The long tables have been set as if we really are waiting on a feast, but I have seen no movement in the kitchens to indicate that this is the case.

Alana enters behind me, barely making a sound.

She is radiant, and almost looks like one of them. Her hair is loose, gathered over one shoulder, with large, beautiful waves that make it shimmer as she moves.

And her dress . . . it is almost like a wedding gown. Long, and silver, and flowing over her curves like it was made for her.

She stands beside me, completely poised.

Her hands are clasped in front of her.

She really is like one of them.

Eldrion enters from the front of the room, appearing from the shadows without warning the way Finn used to. The crowd quiets. This is not the usual way of things.

"Good evening." He addresses them, but he is searching for Alana in the crowd. When he sees her, his eyes flicker with something. Pleasure? Comfort? Relief?

"Thank you for joining us this evening."

Eldrion has barely begun to speak when Alana moves past me, heading straight for him. He notices her and stops talking. The crowd parts for her as she beats her wings, purple magic flickering at their tips.

"I'm afraid" – she raises her voice – "that Lord Eldrion has asked you here under false pretences this evening."

Eldrion stares at her in disbelief and mutters something I can't hear.

She stands right in front of him, blocking him from view with her beauty.

"There is no feast."

Whispers spread through the watching Sunborne. The woman who came to the castle to ask about the storm clouds in the sky steps forward. "My lord, why is this woman speaking for you yet again?"

Before Eldrion can answer, Alana draws herself up taller, tilts her chin, and says, "I am speaking because I have something to say. And you will listen."

Suranna blinks at her incredulously. She raises her hands. Golden magic flickers in them. It is so beautiful I can't look away from it; the Sunborne use their magic sparingly, and I have never seen it before in such close proximity. It changes the air. In an instant, power quivers in every breath.

Another Sunborne steps up beside Suranna and does the same.

Alana studies them, and her eyes twitch at their corners. She is staring at their magic, and in that moment, I know exactly what she is planning to do.

I spin around, heading for the door, but a sudden shaft of purple smoke slams it closed.

The crowd begins to shift, and more Sunborne bring magic into their hands.

The guards try the doors, but Alana's smoke is holding them closed.

"Listen to me, all of you." Alana's voice fills the air. "Eldrion has not told you the truth. What you saw above the castle was the start of something unspeakable. An evil that will destroy this city if we let it."

"What are you talking about?" Suranna spits, her magic still simmering in her hands.

Alana sighs deeply. Behind her Eldrion is watching as if he can't decide whether he is turned on or terrified by what's happening. "It doesn't really matter," Alana says. "I know what will happen if I explain it to you." She beats her wings and rises into the air. "I will tell you what is to come, and you won't believe me. I'll ask you to fight for Luminael, and you'll run. You'll blame me. You'll tell me it is all my fault, and maybe you'll decide that I am the one who should be stopped and not Finn."

"Finn?" Suranna looks at the fae next to her, then back at Alana. "The court jester?" A laugh escapes her lips, then she turns to Eldrion. "Is this some kind of joke, Eldrion? A new act? Because I have to say, I am not finding it very amusing."

Still hovering in the air, Alana's voice cries out. "This is no joke!"

She tips back her head and splays her arms. Her smoke multiplies, sweeping through the grand hall, wrapping itself around the ankles of the Sunborne and the Shadowkind. It grows, and grows.

The Sunborne all summon their magic, but no one attacks her. Not yet.

"Eldrion, do something!" I call to him, but he does nothing. He just watches as Alana's eyes flash bright and violet, and her wings glow.

With a roar, she summons the smoke to her. It rips through the room.

The Sunborne cry and fall to their knees as the smoke envelops them. Their magic continues to glow. Golden, flickering through the smoke. But then it disappears.

The smoke flies back to Alana.

She opens her mouth and screams, and as it enters her she starts to glow. Bright white light surrounds her, illuminating her skin. When she stops screaming, and the smoke dissipates, she is panting, her chest shaking as she breathes. And the Sunborne are on the ground.

Their wings . . .

I look at my own.

They are like me, now.

No longer radiating strength and beauty, but pale and grey. Husks of what they were a few moments ago.

"She took their magic." Kayan is at my shoulder. "She took it from them." He staggers backwards, his own wings fluttering behind him.

Tears are streaming down my face. Suranna is digging her nails into the flagstone floor. She looks up with terrified eyes. Alana looks down at her, and smirks. Her eyes flash golden, then purple, and her wings unfurl, brighter than before. More beautiful.

She lowers herself to the ground and sighs heavily. Then she turns to Eldrion. "Now," she says, "we have all the power we need, and we do not have to rely on anyone but ourselves to win this fight."

He stares at her. I expect to see anger in his eyes, but there is none. A smile parts his lips.

He is proud of her.

Eldrion grabs her waist and kisses her. "What now?" he asks, taking her hand.

"You told me I am not the one in charge," she says, a coy smile on her lips. As if they are alone and no one can hear them.

"It seems I was wrong," he says, stepping back and dipping into a bow. "So, Alana of Luminael. What now?"

Her eyes flicker and she inhales deeply. Pleasure flickers on her skin. "Now," she says. "We rid the city of the remaining Shadowkind. They are who Finn will turn next. We cannot allow him to add to his army."

I look at the guard standing next to me. Pria. She swallows forcefully and bites her lower lip. "You should run," I whisper to her.

She does not turn to face me, but says, "You should, too."

"Oh, I intend to."

TWENTY-SEVEN

Kayan

"*A*lana! This is insanity." I appear in front of her as she storms down the corridor beyond the grand hall. Behind her, she has left the Sunborne fallen and broken.

"I am stopping it," she says, "Now, with my power, I can defeat him, Kayan. I can end this and stop Finn from——"

"End it and be left with what?" I want to shake her, but I can't take hold of her. My voice softens. "Alana, please." I move closer to her. "Look at me." I smile, doing what I can to drag any warm, comforting memories of our time together to the front of her mind.

"I am looking," she says. "And I see a dear friend. The only person who ever truly stood by me."

"That's not true. You have friends, Alana. Rosalie. Briony. We love you."

A look of sadness flickers across her face, but she visibly shakes it away.

Alana moves past me and continues in the direction of the roof. She pauses for a moment, her shoulders shaking. She grips the sides of her head, then inhales sharply. "It's all coming true," she says.

"What is?"

"The visions." She sighs again, and for a moment I think she's going to cry. "There is no point trying to stop it, Kayan. Whatever is destined to be is going to happen. Everything has led here." Her brow furrows. "Perhaps I'm not seeing the future. Perhaps I am creating the future."

This time, I do try to grab her hand. She jumps as if a jolt of static has run through her body. "Alana, you are not creating this. But you do have the power to stop it. Use what you've got to fight Finn, but don't hurt anyone else. Please . . ."

"I think it's time for you to go now, Kayan." She blinks at me with wide eyes, but there is no warmth in them. "I love you, and I miss you, but now it is time for you to leave. Whatever your purpose was here, you've failed. And I do not need you anymore. Go and find Rosalie or go back to the spectral realm you came from." She turns away, looking down at the gold and purple magic in her hands. "Just don't stay here. There is nothing for you here anymore."

"She is right." Eldrion's voice makes me spin around. We have not come face-to-face since the night he held me over the castle and sent me plummeting to my death. He strides towards me and stands close to Alana's side. "There is nothing for you here, spirit." He wraps an arm around her waist. "Your time is over."

Can I really leave her with him?

I back away.

Is this how it ends? With Alana by his side with his evilness inside her?

"Maybe Maura was right," I hear myself whisper.

Alana's back stiffens, but she does not turn around.

"Maybe you really are a monster."

I SHOULDN'T HAVE SAID IT, AND I KNOW I SHOULDN'T. AS I appear in Raine's chambers, and Maura looks up at me from the armchair by the window, she knows instantly that something is wrong.

"What is happening?" she asks quietly. Raine is still sleeping, and the baby is in its crib.

"You need to leave now, Maura."

She looks at Raine, then at the child. "We can't leave, she is not well enough."

"Alana took the Sunborne's magic. She plans to use it to fight Finn, but she just flooded the entire city."

Closing her eyes, Maura presses her lips together. She is not surprised, just resigned.

"You hurt her. We all have. And I'm worried that she is becoming blinded to what is real and what isn't, that she'll give in to the need for vengeance instead of the need to protect the kingdom."

"Kayan, my dear." Maura stands up on thin, fragile legs. "That's already happening."

I dip my head and bite down on the sickening sensations that are swilling in my gut.

"All right. We'll leave. Thank you for warning us."

"Where will you go?"

She tilts her head to the side, then sighs. "I don't know, Kayan. Where should we go? We have no home now. Where is safe?"

"I know a place." The thought forms almost at the same moment it leaves my mouth. "Rosalie."

"Rosalie? The fire fae?"

"She was bought by a lord by the name of Cassius. He has her holed up in a large mansion outside the city, but he . . ." I swallow and look away. "He recently passed away, and Rosalie inherited his wealth."

"He passed away?"

I meet her eyes, and in that moment I know she sees exactly what I did. "He was hurting her."

Maura does not respond, simply nods and strides over to the bed. "Tell me how to get there, and see if you can steal us two horses from the stables. And tell Pen. He's strong enough now. He's in the room down the hall."

I flick my wings, blue light casting shimmering shadows on Maura's face.

"Kayan?" She looks up at me as Raine stirs in the bed. "Thank you."

"We are kin," I tell her. "I will fetch the horses, and I will accompany you to Rosalie's mansion."

"You do not wish to stay with Alana?" Maura asks, helping Raine to sit up.

"Alana is not here anymore, Maura. She's gone." I close my eyes, picture Alana one last time, the way I knew her then, and brace myself to leave her forever.

TWENTY-EIGHT

Eldrion

"What was that?" I storm after Alana. She is heading for the roof, and I have no idea whether I want to rip her clothes off or lock her in chains because of what she has done. "Alana!"

She flicks her wrist out behind her and sends a ball of golden light hurtling towards me, and with it a display of ornate swords falls from the wall, a painting tumbles to the ground, the ceiling shakes.

I cannot even fathom how much power is surging through her right now. The thought of it is too much to comprehend.

The way she is moving. The way she's carrying herself . . . she seems completely unbeatable.

And suddenly, I know without a doubt that no matter how strong Finn's forces are, Alana will win. There is nothing that could be stronger than her.

I catch her arm as we reach the roof. I should probably be afraid of her, but all my body wants is to be close to her.

She swirls around, eyes flashing gold and purple and black, then she releases an almighty scream. She turns her face up towards the storm clouds that are still gathered above the city. And they almost seem to quake under her rage and her elation.

She is smiling when she looks at me. "Can you feel that?" she cries.

I can feel her. She is magical. I am transfixed.

She looks me up and down and her lips curl into a smile. Just the way her eyes move makes me instantly hard.

In an instant, she is in front of me on her knees. She pulls my pants down and takes me in her mouth. "Alana . . ." I don't know why I'm pretending that I want her to stop. I don't. I don't want this to ever stop.

I no longer care about anything but the way her lips feel against my shaft.

I reach down and push her dress from her shoulders. She looks up at me, her eyes still shimmering, her wings out wide behind her back.

Then she stands. "Fly with me," she says, looking up at the storm clouds.

"Fly with you?"

She nods, spreading her wings.

I spread mine too and follow her into the sky. She is heading straight for the centre of the clouds. But still I follow her.

There, she lets her dress fall further, down to her waist. She is treading air with her wings. Lightning crackles around us and she inhales deeply, her entire body vibrating with the power it now contains.

"Fuck me," she says, wrapping her legs around my waist the way we did in the water.

I spin her around roughly, and enter her from behind. Her wings are pressed against me, and she is completely at my mercy.

It is me holding us up.

Only me.

And in that moment, I realise why I find her so irresistible. Why I have always found her irresistible. Because I want to tame her, but I also want her to tame me.

It is an intoxicating dance.

To own something so powerful, and to make her mew and whimper under my touch, fills me with so much heat I can barely breathe.

But for her to own me in return?

She slams back onto me, reaching back to loop her arm around my neck. She comes hard and quickly. There is no romance or love in our fucking. It is a release of pressure. A valve that needs to be loosened. But as we both climax, the lightning intensifies.

Alana barely allows me to finish before she pulls away from me, tugging her dress back up over her breasts and using her wings to keep herself alight in the air.

She looks me up and down approvingly, almost as if she is saying thank you. Then she swoops down from the clouds.

I follow her to the citadel's edge.

Below, the water shimmers beneath the warmth of the deceptively calm sunset.

"What will happen to the Sunborne now?" she asks.

I almost laugh. "You tell me, Alana. What will happen to them?"

"I suppose they will continue as normal. It has been a long time since they used their magic." She tilts her head. "But it will be interesting to see how they change now they do not have the comfort of knowing they are the most powerful fae in the kingdom."

"You are talking as if the battle has already been won and we are living in the after. Finn still needs to be dealt with."

Alana looks at me as though I am a little bit stupid and rolls her eyes. "Of course, but as soon as I have removed his opportunity to grow his forces, he will no longer be a problem for us."

"Removed . . ." I frown at her. "What do you mean?"

She lifts her palms in front of her face. The magic has changed colour. It is blue now, and below us, I feel the tide in the waters around the citadel start to shift.

"Alana, what are you going to do?"

A smile parts her lips. She inhales deeply, then presses her palms outwards as though she is pushing an invisible wall away from herself.

I look away from her, my gaze falling on the now undulating water. It looks as though it is swelling, growing larger, waves crashing against the shore.

"Alana . . ."

"That is the Shadowkind Quarter?" she asks, pointing north.

"It is."

"I will deal with them first, and then we will deal with the ones who are left inside."

I move in front of her, blocking her view, but she closes her eyes as if it makes no difference to what she is doing.

"Those who remain are loyal."

"They are not loyal, and you are a fool if you think they are." Her eyes snap open. "And it does not matter either way. Whether they want it or not, Finn will turn them. So, we need to make sure there is no one here for him to turn."

I beat my wings and turn around. The waves are higher now. She is going to flood the city.

The sky is darkening, angry storm clouds roiling overhead. Lightning flashes, illuminating the scene in stark, purple-white bursts.

Alana is still suspended in the air, her wings spread wide, crackling with power. Her eyes glow an unearthly violet, and her hands are raised above her head.

With a swift, brutal motion, she brings her arms down.

A massive wall of water materialises, towering over the

city's highest spires. For a heartbeat, it hangs there, defying gravity. Then it crashes down.

My vision blurs. I rub my temples as pain stabs the backs of my eyes.

I see what is coming. I have seen it before but now it makes sense.

The wave smashes into Luminael with terrifying force. Buildings crumble like they're made of sand. Streets vanish beneath the deluge. I hear screams, cut short as the water engulfs everything.

The flood races through the city, unstoppable, merciless. Fae of all kinds are swept away, their wings useless against the torrent. The water rises higher and higher, swallowing entire districts in seconds.

The vision fades, leaving me gasping, my heart pounding. I cannot stop it. Alana's wall of water is already gathering pace, moving through the city.

And I have no choice but to let it.

SHE DOES NOT LINGER TO WITNESS THE FRUITS OF HER destruction. Instead she swoops back down to the castle and strides through it as though it belongs to her.

I follow behind, unable to do anything but marvel at her power.

Every Shadowkind we pass, she shoots a bolt of purple smoke towards them. It paralyses them, and then they fall.

They are utterly defenceless. They have no magic, and they do not see their fate coming.

Perhaps they should have, and run when they had the chance.

As each falls, I stare into their vacant eyes and try to decide whether I care that they are dead. If there are feelings present, I can't find them. So, instead, I focus on Alana.

"We should return to the roof and watch for Finn." My wings flick out sideways as I try to keep up with her pace.

"I have somewhere else to go first." She turns a corner. She is heading for the healing wing.

When she reaches it, she goes straight for the door to Raine's room. My breath catches in my chest. She yanks the door open and screams, "Maura! Show yourself."

I wait in the hallway, listening for screams or the sound of a battle.

Nothing comes.

Moments later, Alana marches back into the hall with fury in her eyes and on her skin. "They've gone," she spits. "No matter. After this is over, I will find them."

"She hurt you." I catch Alana's gaze.

"She destroyed me." For a second, just one brief second, hurt swims in her eyes. But then she shakes it off, and the darkness returns.

"But before I can have vengeance, we must destroy Finn."

She stops, as if the momentum in her stride has suddenly begun to waver. She inhales deeply. Is she forcing herself not to think of him? Or is she simply enjoying the raging waves of power that are surging through her body? "You're right," she says. "We should wait on the roof. We are not going to him. He will come to us. And I can't think of a better place to end this. Can you?"

TWENTY-NINE

Briony

_____

*T*he sky is darkening. Grey and purple clouds swarm together above our heads. Thunder rumbles, like the sky is trying to split itself in two. Lightning. Not pale white but bright violet. It streaks across the sky, forking and carving out a path through the clouds.

Behind me, back at the castle, Alana's power swells and grows.

"This is where I leave you." Pria nods at me.

"Where are you going?"

She shakes her head. "No idea, and if I did know, it's not likely I'd tell you." She offers me a firm pat on the shoulder. "Good luck, Briony."

I watch as she leaves, disappearing down a dark alleyway, then quicken my pace. I know where I am heading, and I cannot get there quickly enough.

After winding down several abandoned side streets, I emerge in a small, empty square.

In front of me, the looming facade of an orphanage brings back floods of memories I've tried to forget over the two hundred years since I was released from here into Eldrion's care.

I close my eyes and take a deep breath.

If Alana is coming for the Shadowkind next, they should be warned. And I have to begin here. With the most vulnerable.

I rap on the door firmly with a clenched fist. It swings open to reveal an elderly Shadowkind fae. Black robes, hair pinned back into a tight bun at the base of her neck, thick dark-rimmed glasses.

She clocks my wings, then the sky, then starts to duck back inside, preparing to slam the door in my face.

"Please, wait." I put my foot in the doorway. "Don't shut me out. I'm here to warn you."

Still silent, she folds her arms and narrows her eyes at me.

"There's trouble at the castle. It's hard to explain. But all Shadowkind need to leave the city. Lord Eldrion is coming for us."

I do not mention Alana. It is too much to explain, and her name will not instil as much fear as his.

The Shadowkind fae in front of me nods slowly and looks at the sky again. "I thought as much," she says. Then she steps over the threshold and closes the door behind her.

Pushing past me, she makes her way to the gate.

"Where are you going?" I call, spinning around and hurrying a few steps after her.

"Going to warn my family, of course," she says.

I look back at the building. "What about the children? Who's in charge?"

She stops, tilts her head to the side, and says, "Well, I guess now I'm gone . . . no one." She rolls her tongue over her teeth, then sighs. "They'll have to fend for themselves. I have my own kin to worry about."

And then, just like that, she is gone.

I turn back to the orphanage, push open the heavy wooden door, and step inside. The familiar musty smell hits me immediately – a mixture of old books, dust, and something vaguely medicinal. It's a scent I thought I'd forgotten, but now it rushes back, bringing with it a chilling sense of nostalgia that settles on my skin like ice.

My footsteps echo in the empty hallway as I make my way towards the dormitories. It's late; the children will be in bed.

Each step feels like I'm walking back in time, to when I was just a small, frightened child, thrust into this place with no idea what was going to happen to me or how long I'd be here.

Foolishly, for the longest time, I thought I was here to find parents. A family.

I didn't realise I was here to be prepared for my years of servitude to Eldrion.

I pause outside the dormitory door. Taking a deep breath, I push it open.

The room is dim, lit only by a few flickering candles. Rows of small beds line the walls, each one occupied by a child.

Some are sleeping, others are sitting up, wide-eyed and alert. The sight of them, so vulnerable and afraid, makes my heart ache.

Each has their wings bound.

I swallow hard and try not to notice the bile building in my stomach as I remember exactly what that felt like.

The pain.

The humiliation.

As I step further into the room, another smell reaches me – the faint scent of sage. It's coming from the small sachets hung at the end of each bed, a futile attempt to mask the underlying scent of fear and loneliness that permeates the air.

I remember those sachets. I used to hold mine close at night, breathing in the soothing scent, pretending I was somewhere else, anywhere else.

A small voice breaks through my thoughts. "Who are you?"

I turn to see a young girl, no more than fifty fae years old, staring up at me. The sight of her makes my throat tighten.

"My name is Briony. Your mistress had to leave, but I'm here to take you somewhere safe."

"Safe?" the girl asks.

I crouch down to her level, trying not to terrify her with my version of the truth. "Some bad things are happening in the city, so we need to leave."

"And you're going to help us?" she asks.

"Yes," I manage to say. "I'm here to help." When I stand up, I speak to the rest of the children, projecting my voice to fill the room. "We need to leave, all of us, right now."

As I speak, they begin to stir, whispering amongst themselves. The air in the room shifts, filled with a mixture of hope and fear.

"I know you're scared, and this is a lot to take in," I say, my voice stronger than I feel. "But we have to be brave. And we have to be fast."

Beside me, the girl takes my hand and squeezes it tightly. She is so small, so very small and innocent.

Do Finn and Alana not see what they're doing?

Do they not care how many people they are hurting?

"Will we get out in time?" the girl asks.

It has been a long time since I've been around young fae like this. I've been holed up in Eldrion's castle for most of my life, and it is not a place where children are welcome.

And now here I am, surrounded by them. Trying to get an entire school full of young Shadowkind out of the city before Alana comes for them.

Just thinking those thoughts sends shudders of nausea through me.

When I first met her, she was the most kind and thoughtful person I'd ever encountered. She emanated warmth, and a quiet strength. And there was hurt in her eyes.

She was someone who had seen pain, and hardship, and that was why our bond was so quickly formed.

I brought her into my heart as a friend, and she did the same for me.

At least, I thought she did.

But that Alana has gone.

Maybe she was never really there at all.

She is no different from them now; from Finn, and Eldrion, and all the people who ever made her feel like a monster.

They shaped her in their own image. They turned her into what they feared the most, and now she will destroy us all.

Unless we can get free in time.

"It's going to be all right." I stand at the front of the dormitory and speak loudly. "There's no time to gather any belongings, just get dressed quickly and follow me."

The girl holding my hand, her wings bound tightly to her back, whispers, "We don't have any belongings, miss."

I try to smile at her. "Well then, we'll make this nice and quick, won't we?"

"How are we going to escape?" she asks, blinking at me with wide, blue eyes that remind me of Alana somehow.

I try to shift the thought from my mind.

Alana, the one who is right now plotting to kill every Shadowkind left in the city, is not my Alana anymore. She is a stranger. A monster who has eaten the heart of Alana Leafborne and left darkness in its place. A chasmic black hole that is determined to swallow everything in its path.

"I'm not sure yet." I tweak my fingers under the girl's chin. "But we'll figure something out."

Leaving her to put on her tattered pair of shoes, I wait outside, leaning against the wall, breathing heavily.

I don't know how to do this.

I have no idea how to take a school full of small fae children who can't fly and get them out of the city unseen by Eldrion's forces or by Alana.

The pair of them seem to share his ability to see now. But I don't know what that means. Can they see whatever they want? Will they know that I'm here and what I'm trying to do?

I wring my hands together in front of my stomach. I feel like I might vomit.

In fact, I am going to vomit.

Running over to the garbage can opposite the dormitory, I grip hold of it and vomit hard into its depths. The taste is hot and acrid in my mouth, and leaves me retching and panting for several moments after it's been expelled from my stomach.

When I'm done, I wipe my brow with my forearm and stand up. I straighten my shoulders, push back my wings, and nod determinedly. I can do this. I have no choice. Because I sure as hellfire am not leaving these children to die here.

I turn around, preparing myself to stride back to the door and pull it open with a smile on my face. But I don't need to; they are already standing behind me. Silent and trusting, dressed in their sad grey tunics, they are staring at me.

All twenty of them. Waiting for me to free them from their fate.

"All right, everyone. We're going to move on foot through the city. I know it's going to be scary because you haven't been outside for such a long time. And because bad things have been happening." I draw in a deep breath. "The sky might look a bit scary. But, trust me, if we keep moving, everything will be okay."

No one makes a sound. Except for one small girl who sniffs loudly, already crying with the petrified anticipation of what's to come.

"Everyone pick a buddy and hold hands. You're in charge of your buddy. You keep them next to you always, okay? No one gets left behind."

"What happens when we get out of the city?" asks the girl with the blue eyes.

I force a smile, and try to make it look real. "When we get out of the city, we are free. Easy street," I say, laughing. "And you'll love it. The forests, the lakes. It'll be wonderful."

I try not to think about the fact that Finn and Alana, if they carry on the way they're going, are likely to destroy the entire kingdom. Forests, lakes, everything.

Or wonder whether Alana's hatred of us, and her fear of us, and her newfound desire for vengeance, would see her fury reach beyond the walls of Luminael.

I have to believe it wouldn't.

I have to believe she'd let us go if we made it that far, or that someone else would help us. Surely, if we made it to the mountains, the fae there would not turn away a group of children?

Surely, someone will come to our aid?

THE SKY IS NOW COMPLETELY DARK. A DEEP, VELVETY purple that under any other circumstances would be beautiful – but tonight simply fills me with terror.

As we move through the Shadow Quarter, I expect it to be silent. For everyone to be hiding behind closed doors, shuttered up, sleeping.

But word spreads quickly.

The mistress from the orphanage might not have cared about saving the children in her charge, but she certainly got word out because – all around me – Shadowkind fae are tumbling out of their houses with belongings in makeshift bags and sacks.

Some are trying to load wagons, others are just taking off on foot.

Most are heading for the forests.

But I know what lies there, and I am not taking the children to the scene of Finn's crimes.

No, we are heading for the ocean. We'll cross the bridge that leads away from Luminael, follow the beach along the shoreline, and then go to the mountains.

The mountains feel safe. They feel out of reach, even though I know they are not.

Squeezing the hand of the girl next to me, I lean in to whisper in her ear.

I tell her the plan, and make her promise that if something happens to me, she will help her friends get there. "You just keep on following the shoreline. Do you understand?"

She looks at her friend, a small boy whose hand she's holding. When she looks back at me, she nods. "I understand." The strength in her voice makes me smile.

"Good girl." I stroke her hair. "And when you get to the mountains, you unbind your wings. Do you hear?" I say firmly.

"You'll be with us, though, won't you?" she asks, pushing back her shoulders in an attempt to look brave.

"Of course, I will. This is just in case we get separated." I gesture to her friends. "Now, pass the message along so that everyone knows."

Smiling a little – pleased to be given some responsibility – she does as I've asked and passes the message amongst her friends. It spreads like autumn leaves on a cool breeze. And soon they all look a little brighter.

There is a plan.

They will live happily in the mountains with their unbound wings and the kind mountain fae who take them in.

What a wonderful dream.

I blink tears from my eyes and comb my fingers through my hair.

How did it come to this?

Someone pushes past us, shoving the children out of the way in their hurry to leave the Shadow Quarter. I yell at them, but they don't look back.

Panic is starting to spread.

The bridge is in sight now, and the moon is shining brightly.

"There . . ." I smile and inhale deeply. "We're almost out of the city."

A ripple of excitement spreads through the children and their pace quickens. In their pairs, they scurry onto the bridge. There are a few other Shadowkind heading in this direction, but they do not stop and do not acknowledge me or the children.

No one asks if we need help.

No one questions where we are going.

We are in the middle of the bridge when it starts to shake.

The children stop. Several of them release scared squeaks that sound almost kitten-like in their pitch.

I brace my hand on the side of the bridge and turn back towards the citadel. The castle looms large against the dark sky. A shadow. Barely visible, but beating with a blackness that makes me shudder.

Matching the rhythm of my heart, the bridge shakes again.

The children hurry to the sides and grip on to steady themselves. It creaks.

I peer over the edge. The water is moving faster than it should. Far too fast. As if it can't get back to the ocean quickly enough.

"What's that?" the girl with the blue eyes points in the direction of the castle.

I follow her gaze.

Something is moving towards us. A wall of darkness.

My first thought is of Finn's shadows, but then I realise it is too solid to be shadows. It is not air we are looking at; it is water.

A raging wall of water.

Heading straight for us.

"She's flooding the city," I whisper. "Now the Sunborne are gone, she has no reason not to."

"What's happening?" one of the children cries.

"Run!" I scream at the top of my voice. "Everyone run! Now!"

There is trembling moment of hesitation, and then they do as I say. They run as fast as their small legs can carry them, but it's not fast enough. I spin around to see buildings, and trees, and life being swallowed by the tsunami of liquid hate that is coming for us.

It's going to take us.

It's going to eat us alive.

My wings flutter. But they are not strong enough to fly, and certainly not quick enough to carry twenty children to safety.

Is the bridge strong enough to withstand Alana's flood? I have no idea, but it is our only option.

"Everyone stop! Climb!" I grab the blue-eyed girl and haul her up onto the support beam that rises up and turns into the bridge's large timbre arc. "Climb as high as you can and hang on. Don't let go. Help your friends!"

I run along the bridge, helping each child up so they can grip on and start to climb.

The roar of the flood fills my ears. Cracking, creaking, breaking, the city bends to its will. Surely, the bridge will not survive.

"Hang on! Whatever happens, hang on!" I call, grabbing onto a pillar as the water hits.

It is so loud and so strong that it takes my breath away. The force, the power. I can't breathe. It batters my legs, my stomach, my arms. But it does not reach the children. Not yet.

My hands are growing slick, losing their grip.

"Briony! Climb up! I'll pull you up!" the blue-eyed girl calls, reaching for me.

I can't let go. If I do, that will be it.

"You just hold on!" The water is rising higher. It is so cold. I can't feel my legs or my feet. My hair is plastered against my face. My hand slips. Only one hand remains. I try to dig in my nails, but my fingers are too slick, too weak.

I try.

I try.

And then I fail.

I'm underwater, tumbling in the flood's grip.

My vision starts to darken at the edges.

My last thought before the darkness takes me is a prayer – not for myself, but for Alana. I pray that someday, somehow, she'll find her way back to the light. That she'll remember the person she used to be.

Then the water fills my lungs, and everything fades away.

THIRTY

Finn

We are almost at the castle. Energy and power swells behind me. The Shadowkind and, behind them, the Gloomweavers, who of course joined us without a second thought.

The chance to fight back against Eldrion and allow their most base and disgusting desires to surge to the surface?

They were practically salivating when I offered it to them.

"There is only one condition," I warned them as we left their putrid settlement to the east of Luminael and began our march on Eldrion's city. "No Shadowkind is to be harmed. If you see a Shadowkind fae, you leave them be. Or better yet, you bow and curtsey like the good boys and girls you are."

The Gloomweavers did not appreciate my tone, but they bit their tongues and did not object. The promise of blood is too much for them.

"And what of the Sunborne?" one asked, saliva dribbling onto his bulbous chin.

"Do what you like with them but remember they are powerful. You should use your strength and the element of surprise if you want to overpower them."

"They're powerful," Yarrow says now as we approach the city, "but they're out of practice, Finn. They haven't fought or really used their magic in centuries. They've been sitting pretty, content to let Eldrion fight their battles for them."

"Then let's hope they have forgotten how to fight." I raise my eyebrows at him and grin. He bears the same swirling tattoos of smoke on his skin, but there are fewer of them. He is bigger than me, possibly stronger, but my markings make it clear I am their leader.

And if there is one thing Shadowkind are, it is loyal to one another.

We are not elves or Leafborne. We do not double-cross those who are our kin.

Closing my eyes, I think of Alana.

I cannot wait for her to see what I have built for her. The beauty of the army I am going to lay at her feet. I cannot wait for her to taste the power I am offering her. Because I know she wants it.

Deep down in the basement of her soul, there is a darkness that longs to be in control. She has never had that. I saw it when I let her bind my wings and take me the way she did – the flicker of arousal in her eyes, the joy she felt at being the one to have complete power over another.

I will draw that out of her once more. I will make her see that, by my side, she can have everything she ever dreamed of. I have already killed all those who disrespected her. The Leafborne who pretended to allow her to be one of them but who secretly hated her. Made her feel unworthy. Not good enough.

I will give her the gift of knowing herself, and owning herself. I will set her free, and she will love me for it.

In that moment, I realise that I love her more than I thought I did.

Because now, with every decision I make, I am thinking of her.

In the beginning, I intended to use her. I built up my walls and I delighted in how easily I tricked her into trusting me. But as she trusted me, and I saw who she really was, and how alike we really are, I realised she was the woman I was destined to be with.

My Queen of Shadows.

A smile parts my lips, and Yarrow asks what I'm so happy about.

"The future, my friend. I am happy about the future." I clap his shoulder and he puts his arm around me. His wings beat out behind him, and the look on his face tells me it makes him feel just as jubilant as it makes me feel to finally be able to fly. To be what we were always meant to be.

We have reached the river. I would prefer to be travelling by air, but for stealth, we decided to travel by foot.

At the front of the group, one of the Gloomweavers I asked to scout for us turns and runs back in our direction. He is waving his hands in the air.

"What is it?" My eyes flash and my body coils, ready to fight.

"The river," he pants.

"The river? We're not on a fishing expedition, boy." I push past him and stretch out my wings. I reach the river in seconds, closing the space between the rest of the group and the riverbank.

When I look down, I realise what has made him panic; the water is moving faster than I've ever seen it, and it is so high it looks as though it's about to burst the banks themselves.

Then I see something else.

An arm.

A foot.

A face.

Wings. Tattered, pale wings.

Shadowkind wings.

Yarrow is at my side. He sees what I have seen and he lets out an almighty cry that rattles the trees on either side of the water. "Who did this? Eldrion? He did this?"

I look towards the castle. "This was water magic," I mutter. "This was her."

"Who?"

I meet Yarrow's eyes. "Alana."

Yarrow's voice rises in volume as he draws up in front of me. "Your empath did this? She slaughtered our kind?"

My thoughts are tumbling over one another. They make no sense. None of it makes sense. She wouldn't do that. Yes, she has darkness inside her, but it has not yet been coaxed free, and when it was . . . this was not supposed to happen.

She was supposed to be by my side, not opposite me in battle.

I jump into the water. It rages around my thighs, almost knocking me over, and claws at my wings with its strength. I start to drag the Shadowkind fae from the river.

Yarrow stares down at me.

The others have gathered on the bank, their eyes glowing in the dim evening light.

The Gloomweavers stare, almost bored, completely unaffected. But as I continue to rescue the dead bodies of our kin from the racing water, Yarrow jumps down to help me.

The others do too.

We stand there, as the debris of the city slams into us, trying to knock us from our feet, trying to drag us away with it, and we haul them from their murky fates.

The last body I throw over my shoulder and carry to dry land feels lighter than most of the others. A female.

I lower her to the ground. She has dark hair. It has fallen over her face. I push it free, my heart hammering because I already know who I will see in front of me.

"Briony . . ."

Her eyes are wide and glassy, staring up at the sky. Unblinking.

Her clothes are sodden. Her skin pale.

I lower myself to my knees and try to listen for any signs of breath, even though I know it is futile. Beneath her, her pale wings look almost invisible now they are drenched with river water.

"She's dead, Finn. They are all dead." Yarrow puts a firm hand on my shoulder. I stand up and pace away from the body of my dead friend. I roar and jump up into the sky. Shadows swirl around me. Storm clouds gather. Like the ones over the castle, only darker and more menacing now.

When I return to the ground, I instruct the Gloomweavers to make a funeral pyre and lift the dead Shadowkind onto it. "All except her." I lift Briony into my arms.

Yarrow frowns at me.

"She is a gift. For Alana Leafborne."

THIRTY-ONE

Alana

My eyes are fixed on the horizon. The wind whips around me, tugging at my hair and clothes, but I barely notice. My attention is entirely focused on the approaching storm. It is gathering just beyond the city, except the city no longer looks like a city. It is almost completely flooded. Spires and rooftops are just visible, some trees, and the remains of the bridge beyond the Shadowkind Quarter.

I sigh with relief as I look at it.

Barely a soul can have survived.

Finn is approaching, but there is nothing here for him to take or twist.

The only thing waiting for him is me. And my wrath.

I study the storm.

At first, it looks like just another bank of dark clouds. But then I realise it is moving.

Next to me, completely silent, Eldrion unfurls his fading wings and studies it too.

It draws nearer, and I start to make out shapes within the roiling mass. Wings. Bodies. An army.

"This is it. He's here." I look at Eldrion. "The Sunborne?"

"Safe in the grand hall."

"The remaining Shadowkind?"

"Locked in the dungeons with the elves." He tilts his head. "I thought you wanted to end them all. Now."

"I do. But I thought about what you said. About not giving into anger."

He frowns at me.

"I am waiting to see if my anger subsides." I wait a beat, then laugh loudly. "They are my backup plan. If Finn knows they are there, he will want to free them."

"A trap?" Eldrion smiles at me. "A trap," he repeats.

I look back up at the sky and my breath catches in my throat as I spot him at the forefront. Finn. Even from this distance, I can see how he's changed. His wings are massive, pitch black and seeming to absorb the light around them. Shadows swirl around his form, occasionally coalescing into ethereal shapes before dissipating again.

Behind him, a sea of transformed Shadowkind fills the sky. Their wings beat in unison, creating a sound like distant thunder. Some bear the same shadow markings as Finn, while others seem to shimmer with a dark, shadow-like sheen.

I see one of them look down at the ground and follow their gaze to the eastern edge of the city. Gathered at the archway, picking their way through the debris in the places where the flood has receded a little, are the creatures I hoped I would never see again.

Gloomweavers

As they draw closer, I can make out more details. The Shadowkind's eyes glow with an unnatural red light. The Gloomweavers leer and gnash their teeth, clearly eager for the coming battle even though there is barely anyone left to fight, and by the time they reach the castle, it will all be over.

"You should join the other Sunborne," I tell Eldrion.

"Hide? You want me to hide?"

"It is for the best." I put a hand on his forearm. "You have no power, Eldrion."

"I am not leaving you." He straightens his shoulders. "And besides, we are going to take back my power. Remember?" He fixes his gaze on mine as though he can tell I am considering my options.

"I remember." I squeeze tightly. "But then stay behind me and let me deal with this."

I watch them approaching, and try to latch on to the sensations rolling through my body. Power and adrenaline. Not fear.

Fear is nowhere to be found.

Only a visceral need to end this, and to show everyone what I am capable of.

How much they underestimated me.

How foolish they were.

Finn flies slightly ahead of the others, very clearly their new leader. The shadows around him seem to pulse with every beat of his wings. His eyes, when I can finally see them clearly, are fixed directly on me.

I almost smile as he draws closer. I feel as though I have been waiting for this moment for all my life: the chance to unleash what has been buried for so many years.

I take a deep breath, steeling myself for what's to come.

Because it is going to be so very good.

"Alana!" he calls down to me. He is carrying something. A large, dark bundle in his arms.

He stops above me, treading the air. His army stops too, glaring down at us.

The bundle falls. He lets it tumble. It hits the ground in front of me with a thud that sends a jolt of nausea through me. I see dark hair, and pale skin, and the wings of a Shadowkind.

I move forward and crouch down.

"Alana, don't." Eldrion warns me to stop, but I ignore him. As I push her hair aside, my breath catches in my chest and my vision blurs.

I'm standing in the streets of Luminael, but they're unrecognisable. Water rushes through them like raging rivers, swallowing everything in its path. Water I conjured. Destruction I invited.

Buildings crumble, debris floats by, and the screams of the desperate and dying fill the air.

Through the chaos, I spot a familiar figure . . . Briony. She's clinging to a piece of floating wreckage, her wings waterlogged and useless. Her face is a mask of terror as she fights against the current.

"Help!" she screams, her voice barely audible over the roar of the flood. "Please, someone help!"

I try to move towards her, to reach out, but I'm frozen in place, forced to watch helplessly.

Around her, small Shadowkind fae, young ones, so young, cling to the bridge and call out for Briony. She tells them to stay strong.

But then a massive wave crashes over her, submerging her completely. And when the water recedes, she's gone. My heart clenches as I search frantically for any sign of her.

Then I see her, carried swiftly away by the merciless current. Her body tumbles through the water, limp and lifeless. Her eyes are open, staring blankly at nothing.

She is gone.

I killed her.

I cry out in pain and scramble backwards, my heart racing, my breath shaking in my chest.

Eldrion is at my side, towering above me, but he can do nothing to protect me, and Finn's army is coming for me.

THIRTY-TWO

Finn
<hr style="width: 15%;" />

I have broken her, and I am glad of it. A moment ago, she was so strong and so very cocky. And now she is like a scared child, scrambling away from the body of her dead friend. Her only friend.

"Seek out the Sunborne and end them," I tell Yarrow. "Don't stop until they are all gone."

He nods at me. "You'll handle the empath?"

"I'll handle the empath." I stare down at the roof. "And the Fae Lord."

As my army disappears, swooping down to scour the flooded streets and buildings, and the dark crevices inside the castle walls, I land on the edge of the roof.

So much has happened here. This very spot is where Kayan had his wings ripped from his back. This is where I transformed, and now this is where it will all end.

"I really did want you to be by my side at the end of this." I jump down onto the roof, my feet landing with a heavy thud. "But after what you did to my kind, I am not sure there is any way back for us."

Alana looks up at me. Tears are streaming down her cheeks. "I did not do this." She gestures to Briony. "None of this would have happened if it wasn't for you."

"No, Alana. You did this. You chose to destroy hundreds of fae to save yourself."

"That's not true."

"It *is* true!" I bellow. "You got high on the power. You were enjoying it. I saw it in your eyes and your body in those moments before I dropped Briony at your feet. Before you saw the evidence of your own evil intent."

"Everything I have done has been to protect this city from you."

"And who do you sound like now?" I am standing above her. Eldrion tries to step in my way, but I push him over with just one jerk of my wrist. The once powerful lord goes flying towards the wall and crashes into it, falling to the floor in time for my shadows to begin swirling at his feet.

He cries out. I stifle his noise with more darkness.

Alana looks at him, then at me. She stares into my eyes, and I blink down at her. "I think we can overcome it," I whisper. "If you apologise and promise to be a good girl from now on."

She lowers her gaze.

There it is. She is mine again.

But then she looks up at me. Gold and purple flicker in her gaze. Her wings spread wide and she rises to her feet. She pulls back her arm and, without hesitation, hurls a bolt of magic towards me.

And the power of it . . .

I am almost impressed when it hits me in the chest and sends me flying.

What is this? It is not just her magic and the water magic she stole from Kayan, it is something greater than that, too.

"What did you do?" I ask, tilting my head in awe as she stalks towards me.

"You are not just dealing with one person's power now, Finn," she says. "I have the power of an entire city inside me. And you're about to know what it feels like when it takes everything you have, and turns it to ash inside your bones."

I grin at her, rising to my feet.

"I cannot wait," I tell her.

THIRTY-THREE

Alana

I stand before Finn, my body thrumming with power. The magic of hundreds of fae courses through my veins, a symphony of elements and abilities all singing for release. It's intoxicating, overwhelming, and for a moment, I understand how Finn could have lost himself to this feeling. I think I am losing myself, too.

But I no longer care.

Caring hurts too much.

Flinging an arm out behind me, I send Briony's body up into the air. It hovers for a moment, and then I throw her over the edge of the roof.

She is gone, now.

And so am I.

Finn rises up, his red eyes flashing. Behind me, Eldrion cries out. I do not need to watch him to know that the shadows are taking him.

It is as though all the visions I've ever had are living in my head now at the same time as what is real, and happening. I can see everything.

I can see Finn's army of Shadowkind attacking the castle, battering down the doors of the grand hall and attacking the Sunborne who are huddled there.

I can see the Gloomweavers turning to looting and pillaging because there are not enough fae left in the city to kill.

And I can see what is happening behind me. Even as I focus on Finn and the dark, inky black magic that is coiling around his forearms, ready to attack, I can see Eldrion.

At first, it's subtle – wisps of darkness curling around his ankles, almost playful in their movements. But then they start to climb.

The shadows slither up his legs, wrapping around him like inky tendrils. Eldrion's eyes widen in panic, his hands clawing at the darkness as if trying to peel it off. But his fingers pass right through, unable to grasp the intangible threat.

"Alana!" he cries out, his voice strained. "Do something!"

His wings begin to twitch and spasm as the darkness envelops them. Eldrion's face contorts in pain, a silent scream etched across his features.

The shadows reach his neck, curling around his throat like a noose. I can see the struggle in his eyes, the fight to breathe as the darkness tightens its grip.

Finally, the shadows engulf him completely. He is totally

obscured, a silhouette of pure darkness against the backdrop of the castle.

I roar loudly and thunder crackles in the air above us. It begins to rain. I call for it, for the water that will slick the roof and our skin.

Finn sends his shadow magic snaking out towards me. Vipers of blackness, slithering, coiling, coming for me.

I pull my own magic into my hands and throw a few bolts of smoke in his direction. But I have no intention of stopping him. I let the shadows come for me. I back away, allowing the illusion of fear to enter my eyes.

Finn tilts his head. "There is still time to change your mind, Alana. Say the word and this all stops."

I am beside Eldrion now, pushed up against the wall. I reach for his hand and grab hold of it as shadow and smoke consumes me the way it consumed him.

I let it enter my body. I feel it race through my veins and tighten around my bones, its vice-like grip squeezing and squeezing until I can barely breathe.

It is trying to suffocate my other powers, stamp them out, extinguish them.

But that is as far as it will go.

With a scream that Finn interpret as pain, I let the gates down in my mind and I suck those shadows further and further into my soul. I keep pulling.

Now Finn is screaming. When I open my eyes, his body is being dragged towards me by an invisible force. Shadows fly from his chest, and his mouth, and his eyes. His wings beat as if they are being tossed around by a storm.

He tries to fight it, but he can't. And then realisation dawns in his dimming eyes.

No longer bright red.

Darker.

Greyer.

Like his wings.

"Take them from him, Alana," I hear Eldrion whisper beside me, and I let out another cry. I break free from the shadows that bound me, and now I am the one wielding them. I wear them like jewellery, watching them form dark rings of power around my arms, overwhelming the light and the elemental magic I had consumed from Kayan and the Sunborne.

Overtaking everything.

As I move towards Finn, more shadows come.

There are screams, and the sound of Finn's army trying to resist me.

I can see them too, being dragged from the grand hall, unable to stop themselves being taken by me.

I see the Sunborne gathered together like scared children, confused and sobbing with relief as their attackers are hauled with brutal strength away from them, through the large glass windows, their skin and wings torn and bleeding.

I bring them to me. All of them. And one by one they fall at my feet.

They writhe on the ground, the way the Leafborne did when they were taken from me.

They try to escape, try to crawl away, but I do not let them.

"Alana. Let me help." Eldrion is free now too, and striding towards me. I hurl some of his magic back towards him and he sucks in a huge, deep breath as it reunites with his body. His wings are instantly back to the way they were. Huge, bright, powerful.

He strides forward and reaches out with his hands.

While I focus on Finn, he moves towards Yarrow. He stands above him and hauls him to his feet. Yarrow does a good job of fighting back. He is strong. He tries to batter the shadows, tries to resist as they clamp down on his mouth and enter his nose, choking the breath from his body.

He mutters Finn's name, but Finn cannot help him now.

And then he falls.

They all fall.

I hold Finn still in my shadowy grasp and I make him watch. A tear rolls down his cheek. I lean in and catch it with my index finger. "Don't cry, jester. Your turn will come. You will not have to live with this pain much longer."

He whispers my name, and keeps whispering it until the last of his army has breathed their final breath.

As Eldrion staggers to the edge of the roof, panting, glistening with power once again, I make Finn stand and face me.

He is cocooned in my shadows. *My* shadows.

I stare into his eyes, and reach into his mind. For a moment, I soothe him. I latch onto his pain and I lessen it. Soften it. Kiss it better with my thoughts. And then I take away the comfort and replace it with something else.

Memories.

The first time we met in Eldrion's castle, my fear giving way to curiosity as Finn showed me kindness.

Laughter echoing through the corridors as Finn taught me to juggle, his eyes sparkling with mischief.

Late-night conversations, sharing our hopes and fears, feeling understood for the first time in years.

The warmth of Finn's hand in mine as we plotted our escape, a promise of freedom and a better life.

The exhilaration of flying together, wings finally unbound, the world stretching endlessly before us.

But then the memories darken. And I show him what he did to me, and what he made us become.

The first time I saw a flicker of something sinister in Finn's eyes, quickly masked but unforgettable.

The moment I realised Finn had been manipulating me all along. The pain I felt. I give it to him, I make him feel it, too.

Watching in horror as Finn transformed, shadows consuming the man I thought I knew. I give him that horror. I stare into his eyes as it blooms in his gut, and flames of guilt and fury lick at his insides.

I let him feel what I felt looking at Briony, and what I felt when my own kind turned against me, and what I felt when Eldrion fucked me.

Finn is writhing in my grasp.

I give him my pain. All of it, so that I do not have to live with it a second longer.

And when he is full to the edges, and cannot take anymore, I whisper. "Thank you, Finn. You created me. And I really do like what I have become."

He tries to speak. But I am done.

I squeeze his final breath from his body then I let him fall to the ground.

Lying there now, he looks just as he did before. His body is smaller, and his wings are pale.

He looks completely harmless.

But looks can be deceiving, can't they?

Eldrion steps over the bodies of Finn's army and takes my hand. "He's gone," he says, studying my face as though he is waiting for me to dissolve into tears.

I let go of him and pace to the edge of the roof. Darkness is descending on the city, now.

And it feels like home.

"Alana." Eldrion stands beside me. "My magic."

"I returned it to you," I say calmly, lacing my fingers together behind my back.

"Not all of it," he replies darkly.

I turn to look at him and hold his gaze for a long time. "No, not all of it." I press my lips to his and kiss him deeply. "I think it's best I keep a little back for now, don't you?"

I do not give him the chance to reply.

I leave him on the roof and soar up into the sky. To survey what is now, and forever, mine.

THIRTY-FOUR

Eldrion

_____

*H*er form appears at the foot of the bed. Alana is sleeping. I get up slowly and move to the window. She follows me.

"What do you want, mother?"

She does not speak.

"Have you come to tell me how proud you are? To thank me for saving our kingdom?"

She closes her eyes. A tear escapes and falls down her cheek, and as it runs down her perfectly smooth skin, it drags a pang of anger from my gut.

"Why are you crying? It worked. You created Alana to save us, and she saved us."

My mother shakes her head. Her long, silver hair is loose over her shoulders. Usually, she wears it tied up in intricate braids. But she looks different today. "She condemned you," she whispers.

I look over at the bed. Alana is sleeping with one wing unfurled behind her and one arm up over her head. Her hair splays out across the pillow. She looks like an angel. A fiery angel.

"She took your power."

"She gave it back."

"Not all of it."

"I cannot blame her for that. Why would she trust me?"

"She destroyed everything." My mother's wings droop, and her shoulders fall with them. "I was wrong, Eldrion. And I am so sorry."

"You were not wrong, mother. For once, you were right. And I want to thank you."

She is crying now. Tears streaming from her eyes. And I hate her for it. Why is she so weak? Now, of all times, when we have taken back what is ours and can protect it for centuries to come. For millennia. When no one will be able to threaten our peace ever again.

"Do not let that devil sleep in your bed, son. Find a way to free yourself from her. Promise me."

"I will make you no such promise."

When I look back at the bed, Alana is sitting up, watching us. She tilts her head to the side. "The Lady of Luminael," she breathes.

She rises quickly and crosses the room as though she is going to pull my mother into a tight embrace. She is wearing a long, flowing white nightdress. It billows behind her as she moves.

But when she reaches us, she stops and opens her palm. Her magic flickers. Her eyes flash. "How dare you show yourself to me?" she asks quietly, firmly, with a level of control that sends shockwaves of pleasure through my entire body. "You are not welcome here."

"I created you," my mother says, drawing closer to Alana.

"Yes, you did. But it is time for you to go, now."

"You are a monster."

Alana tilts her head and sighs. "I am so very tired of hearing that," she says. Then she throws a ball of swirling light, and shadow, and magic towards my mother. It circles her throat, and her eyes widen.

"You didn't think a spirit could be choked?" Alana asks, stalking towards my mother like an animal stalking its prey. "My spirit was choked for years, and years, and years. Until I finally took back control and set myself free."

My mother reaches up with shaking hands, trying to pry the shadows from her throat.

"I am the Lady of Luminael now," Alana says. "And you are no longer welcome here."

She stands back and flicks her wrist.

And just like that, my mother is gone.

The shadows consume her in seconds. Her legacy, her judgement, her hatred, her cowardice. Gone.

When I turn to Alana, she is smiling. I wrap my arms around her waist and turn her face up to mine, kissing her with a fury that makes my wings shudder. "Thank you," I whisper into her lips.

"What for?" she asks, stepping back and dropping her nightdress to the floor.

"For having the power to rule us all." I grab her and lift her into my arms.

"Thank you for coaxing it free." She stares into my eyes. "It was always meant to be this way." She presses her palm to my chest. "We are the same, Eldrion. You and I."

"Yes." I lay my hand on top of hers. "Yes, we are."

THIRTY-FIVE

Rosalie

―――――――――

*T*he knock at the door startles me, even though it is not the first to have come in the middle of the night. I was not sleeping, just sitting by the fireplace remembering.

It has become a dangerous habit lately, to sit and remember the way things used to be instead of thinking about the way things are now.

As soon as the battle was over, and the sky returned to normal, it was tempting to feel as though we were safe.

Mira brought word from the city. When she told me what Alana had done, I could hardly bring myself to believe it. And yet, somehow, I was not surprised. It felt as though, maybe, everything had always been leading up to this.

I saw Alana the way I had always seen her in my mind's eye, but then I saw her through a different lens. One that showed every slice of pain that was ever inflicted on her, showed her tossed and turned in the wind of others' wants and fears.

She didn't stand a chance.

And neither did we.

I am only pleased Kayan is not here to see what became of her. Because it would break his heart the way it breaks mine.

When I reach the door, I hesitate, my hand hovering over the handle.

"My lady?" a small voice pipes up behind me. I turn to see Lily, the blue-eyed child who arrived on my doorstep just days ago, seeking sanctuary with her friends. "Should I hide?"

I smile reassuringly at her. "No need, little one. Stay close, though."

Taking a deep breath, I open the door, expecting to see more orphans or waifs or strays because Mira has been passing word that our home is safe.

Whether it truly is or not, I don't know. But for now, Alana seems to be leaving us alone.

I waver and steady myself on the doorframe.

I turn back towards the inside of the house, wondering if I'm somehow walking in my sleep. Dreaming while awake.

I physically pinch my arm and wince at the pain.

"Kayan?" I whisper. "Kayan?" I repeat his name like a prayer.

He smiles at me. His hair is the same, his lips, his eyes, his cheeks. But he is different somehow. His skin has a blueish tint to it and his wings . . . I have not seen them like that since before Alana took his powers.

Beside him, Maura, Raine, and Pen smile at me too.

"It is very good to see you, child." Maura moves forward and wraps me in a tight embrace.

But my focus is entirely on Kayan. Without thinking, I move aside from Maura and reach out to him.

"Are you really here?"

"Not really," he says. "I'm . . ."

"A spirit," Raine offers. "From what we can work out."

"How?" I move my fingers towards him.

To my shock, my hand doesn't pass through him. Instead, I feel the solid warmth of his chest beneath my palm. A jolt of energy passes between us, like a current of pure emotion.

Kayan inhales sharply. "I feel you," he breathes.

"I feel you, too."

"Rose." Kayan's eyes soften.

Unable to hold back any longer, I throw myself into his arms. He catches me, his embrace as strong and comforting as I remember. Tears stream down my face as I cling to him, breathing in his familiar scent.

"How are you here?" I whisper, picturing the torn remains of his portrait. Still in my dresser upstairs.

Kayan's arms tighten around me. I still feel him, and I have no idea how. "It's complicated," he says softly. "But I'm here now. And we're here because we need your help, Rose. Luminael isn't safe for us. Can we stay here?"

"Of course, you can."

A shadow passes over Kayan's face. "Things have . . . changed, Rose. Alana's not the same person we knew. The power she's gained, it's . . ."

"I know. I've heard the stories."

"She flooded the city." Lily, the tiny Shadowkind girl, speaks up from behind me. Her blue eyes glisten. "We nearly drowned."

"You poor child." Maura steps towards Lily and places a kind hand on the girl's shoulder. "But you made it out and made it here. Well done."

"A lady helped us," she says. "A lady called Briony. She was kind. She had black hair. But she died."

Kayan and Maura exchange a look that tells me they know exactly who Briony was.

I want to ask them about it, but now is not the time.

I straighten up, wiping my tears away. "Come in," I say, stepping back to allow them entry. "All of you. Tell me everything."

As the group files past me into the hall, my hand finds Kayan's again. Our fingers intertwine, and that same spark of energy passes between us. I'm not letting go of him again. Never. Not ever.

"Was it you?" I ask as we walk slowly down the hall.

He looks down at me.

"Did you drown my husband, Kayan? And did you visit me in my bed? And by the fountain?"

He does not smile, but nods at me, holding my gaze. "Yes. The answer to all of those questions is yes."

I breathe in deeply, remembering his touch, and the way it felt when I woke up and learned Cassius was dead. As if a guardian angel was looking after me. "Thank you."

"I would do anything for you, Rose."

"Don't ever leave me again."

"I promise."

In front of us, Lily is leading Maura and the others into the kitchen and offering to make them tea, and fetch them food, and find clean clothes. She looks at Raine's arms and gasps when she realises she's holding a baby.

Raine sits down at the table, and her entire body seems to relax.

"For now, they are safe." I keep hold of Kayan's hand.

"For now," he says. "But I don't know how long we have. Alana can't be trusted. She has too much power, now. And the empathy she was born with? That was supposed to save us? It has turned to ice in her veins, Rosalie."

"Do you think she will come for us?"

He squeezes my hand tighter. But he doesn't answer me.

He doesn't need to.

I already know the answer.

Epilogue

The Prophecy of Flame and Shadow

In the annals of the ancient elves, kept hidden for millennia in the deepest recesses of their sacred libraries, there exists a prophecy. Written in shimmering ink that seems to dance on the page, it speaks of a time when darkness will engulf the land, and hope will come in the form of fire.

The prophecy reads thus:

When shadows lengthen and night holds sway, when water drowns and light gives way, a queen of darkness shall arise, her power blackened, her heart of ice.

With stolen magic, she'll remake the world, into a realm of shadows unfurled. The old order toppled, the balance undone, a new age of darkness will have begun.

But hope remains, a spark in the gloom, a child of flame to seal the doom, of she who sits upon shadow's throne, fire shall come to claim its own.

Born of embers, raised in strife, this chosen one shall bring new life. With wings of flame and heart of gold, the fire fae's tale shall be told.

Through trials of pain and loss they'll grow, their power building, their spirit aglow. When all seems lost, when hope burns low, the fire fae's true strength shall show.

In combat fierce, they shall collide, shadow and flame, darkness and light. The fate of all shall hang in the balance, as fire meets shadow in a deadly dance.

And so, the fae realm waits and watches, poised on the brink of a conflict that will shape the future of their world. The time of the prophecy is at hand. The reign of shadow has begun.

But fire is rising to meet it.

Join ALexis Brooke's Newsletter

Join Alexis Brooke's newsletter and stay uptown date on any upcoming releases HERE

Printed in Great Britain
by Amazon

62496194R00161